ELITE AMBITION

Other books in the
CANTERWOOD CREST SERIES:

TAKE THE REINS

CHASING BLUE

BEHIND THE BIT

TRIPLE FAULT

BEST ENEMIES

LITTLE WHITE LIES

RIVAL REVENGE

HOME SWEET DRAMA

CITY SECRETS

CANTERWOOD CREST

ELITE AMBITION

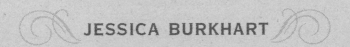
JESSICA BURKHART

m!x

ALADDIN M!X

New York London Toronto Sydney

This book is a work of fiction. Any references to historical events, real people, or real locales are used fictitiously. Other names, characters, places, and incidents are the product of the author's imagination, and any resemblance to actual events or locales or persons, living or dead, is entirely coincidental.

ALADDIN M!X
Simon & Schuster Children's Publishing Division
1230 Avenue of the Americas, New York, NY 10020
First Aladdin M!X edition September 2010
Text copyright © 2010 by Jessica Burkhart
All rights reserved, including the right of reproduction in whole
or in part in any form.
ALADDIN is a trademark of Simon & Schuster, Inc., and related logo
is a registered trademark of Simon & Schuster, Inc.
ALADDIN M!X and related logo are registered trademarks
of Simon & Schuster, Inc.
For information about special discounts for bulk purchases, please contact
Simon & Schuster Special Sales at 1-866-506-1949 or
business@simonandschuster.com.
The Simon & Schuster Speakers Bureau can bring authors to your live event. For
more information or to book an event contact the Simon & Schuster Speakers
Bureau at 1-866-248-3049 or visit our website at www.simonspeakers.com.
Designed by Jessica Handelman
The text of this book was set in Venetian 301 BT.
Manufactured in the United States of America 0516 OFF
8 10 9 7
Library of Congress Control Number 2010929466
ISBN 978-1-4424-0382-6
ISBN 978-1-4424-0383-3 (eBook)

No one else deserves a dedication more than Kate Angelella,
who kept me semisane through a twelve-hour writing marathon and
didn't leave when I threw a lip gloss. . . .

ACKNOWLEDGMENTS

To everyone on Team Canterwood at Simon & Schuster including: Fiona Simpson, Bethany Buck, Liesa Abrams, Mara Anastas, Lucille Rettino, Bess Brasswell, Venessa Williams, Katherine Devendorf, Ellen Chan, Alyson Heller, Jessica Handelman, Karin Paprocki, Russell Gordon, and Dayna Evans.

Alyssa Henkin, thank you for taking the first step toward Canterwood.

Editor K (a.k.a. Kate Angelella), you fueled me through the final steps of writing and your notes made it über-sparkly. P.S. I loved our reward system for this book and will only work under those conditions in the future. ☺

Reader girlies, huge hearts to all of you for chatting on the forums, creating graphics, and cheering me on while I write.

Ross Angelella, thanks for saying you'd leave work in the middle of the day to shake me if you found out I was writing when I obviously needed a break.

Thanks so much to all of my writer friends who offer support and encouragement.

Kate Angelella, for the five fifteen a.m. roller derby–esque walks ("Oscar!"), "I know it's a flower, but . . . ," equal opportunity mocking, and for scaring the "what?" and "huh?" out of my vocabulary. LYSSMB.

ELITE AMBITION

I

DEAR SASHA

9/19/10 11:15am

To: Jacob Schwartz (gamerguy@zahoo.com)

From: Sasha Silver (sassysilver@mymail.com)

Subject: Hey

Hi Jacob,

I can't stop thinking about you, so I wanted to e-mail and say hi. It's only the first day of fall break, but I miss seeing you around. I know things are messed up between us and this e-mail probably doesn't help, but I wanted to be honest. Hope you're doing okay after the Homecoming dance.

~Sasha

PS: My phone broke and I won't get it back till the week-end, so don't try to text me. E-mail me back—if you want.

9/19/10 4:32pm
To: Sasha Silver (sassysilver@mymail.com)
From: Jacob Schwartz (gamerguy@zahoo.com)
Subject: re: Hey

Sasha—
I didn't expect you to e-mail me at all. I'm really glad you did. I know you said you want to stay single. I respect that and I won't push you anymore. But I miss you—I'm not going to lie, especially since we're both being honest about this.
Jacob

9/20/10 7:32am
To: Jacob Schwartz (gamerguy@yahoo.com)
From: Sasha Silver (sassysilver@hotmail.com)
Subject: re: re: Hey

That's kind of why I was e-mailing. I'm just so confused. I know I keep sending mixed signals. I get that. And I don't

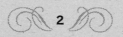

2

want to hurt Callie or cause drama. But . . . never mind. Hope you're having a good break.

~S

9/20/10 6:25pm

To: Sasha Silver (sassysilver@mymail.com)

From: Jacob Schwartz (gamerguy@zahoo.com)

Subject: re: re: re: Hey

You can't leave things hanging like that. Just say it—whatever it is. Do you want me to call you or something? Someone told me you were staying with Heather. Maybe I could call you on her phone.

Jacob

9/21/10 10:15am

To: Jacob Schwartz (gamerguy@yahoo.com)

From: Sasha Silver (sassysilver@hotmail.com)

Subject: re: re: re: re: Hey

No, don't call. It's too hard to talk about this over the phone. Okay . . . fine. I'll tell you. I liked Eric. A lot. But now, I hope we can stay friends and that's it. And I know you had feelings for Callie. But I've been thinking about

*what you said that we never got a chance to really try be-
ing boyfriend and girlfriend. If you want, could we meet
at the fountain when we get back to school? I still want
to be careful not to hurt anyone, but maybe we owe it to
ourselves to at least talk.*

~S

9/21/10 1:08pm
To: Sasha Silver (sassysilver@mymail.com)
From: Jacob Schwartz (gamerguy@yahoo.com)
Subject: re: re: re: re: re: Hey

*Sash, I never want to hurt Callie either. And I don't want you
to feel guilty about Eric, but like you said—you've moved on
and I believe you when you say you want to be his friend. I
think we should definitely meet when we get back to campus. Let's talk about this before things get crazy with school.
I can't wait to see you.*

Jacob

As if I'd needed to read those e-mails again. I folded the
papers and looked out window of Heather's Lincoln Town
Car. The driver, Paul, pulled up to campus. Heather stared
out the opposite window. We'd barely said a word to each

other during the car ride from her New York City penthouse to Canterwood Crest Academy.

I stuck the papers in my purse and rubbed my eyes. For the entire fall break, Heather had been e-mailing Jacob as me. When I'd found out last night, I'd lost it over what she'd done.

This morning, I'd expected to wake up hating her. She'd hacked into my e-mail account, wrote my almost ex–boyfriend, and had arranged for Jacob and "me" to meet at the fountain at school. Heather hadn't apologized. She said she'd given me options—I could meet Jacob or not.

The choice was mine.

I'd been *furious* in that moment and had been in a panic about what I'd do when we got back to school.

But when I'd woken up, I hadn't hated Heather. She was *Heather Fox* after all and that's how she handled situations. She took control and tried to solve problems the "Heather" way, even if they weren't hers to fix. I'd known that about her for a long time. As I'd finished packing this morning, I kept waiting for the rush of anger. But that never happened.

I had to admit the truth to myself. Heather had been right last night when she'd said by e-mailing Jacob, she'd done what I couldn't. She'd told him exactly how

I was feeling and nothing she'd e-mailed him had been a lie. Heather had told him everything I'd been too scared to think about, let alone e-mail to Jacob. Last night, I hadn't decided whether I was going to meet Jacob or not, but this morning, I'd known exactly what I was going to do.

Heather hadn't asked for my answer.

Paul eased the car up the winding driveway and passed rows of dark-railed fences that kept bay, black, gray, and other beautiful horses from roaming free. Even though I'd only been away for a week during fall break, the beauty of the campus almost made me press my nose to the glass. I wanted to take in every inch of the gorgeous Connecticut campus.

Sometimes, I still couldn't believe that I—a small town girl from Union, Connecticut—had been accepted to one of the most prestigious boarding schools on the East Coast. Not only was Canterwood *insanely* tough academically, but it also boasted a top-notch equestrian program. Thinking about riding made me miss my horse, Charm, so much that I almost wanted to climb out of the moving car and run toward the stable.

I frowned.

Before I could do that, I'd have to go back to my room

and face a situation I'd been avoiding for the entire fall break—my falling out with Paige at the Homecoming dance that had caused me to stay at my former arch-nemesis's penthouse, instead of getting the planned break with my BFF/roomie.

2

BFF . . . RIGHT?

"THANKS AGAIN FOR EVERYTHING," I SAID TO Paul. I hugged him and he gave me a warm embrace back.

"It was my pleasure," he said, unloading the last of Heather's and my suitcases from the car. "I hope you visit again."

He hugged Heather, too, and got into the car. Heather and I watched the car disappear down the driveway, then looked at each other.

"So, do you still totally hate me for e-mailing Jacob?" Heather asked. Her blue eyes stayed on my face. A light September breeze blew back her blond hair and she folded her arms across her long-sleeve hunter green shirt.

"No," I said. "I hate what you did. But I do believe you

were trying to help. You went about it the wrong way, but it wasn't because you were trying to mess up things any more than they already are with Jacob and me."

I tucked back strands of my own golden-brown hair. Heather shifted, taking a breath.

This morning, I'd just thrown on old jeans, a T-shirt, blue hoodie, and sneakers. I was saving my new Manhattan clothes from our shopping spree for when school officially started tomorrow. But Heather looked back-to-school ready in skinny jeans and peep-toe wedges.

"Let's get one thing clear," Heather said. "I didn't do it to be nice. I did it because you helped me to talk to Troy." She paused, looking at the gravel driveway. "It would have taken me forever to do that on my own. I owed you. So don't get all gross and gushy on me."

"Well, whatever your reasons—thanks." I thought for a minute. "I know what I have to do now."

Heather popped up the handle of her suitcase and looked at me. "What's that?"

"I'm going to the fountain."

Together, Heather and I rolled our luggage up the sidewalk until we got to the spot where we needed to split to get to our dorms—Winchester and Orchard. Heather hadn't asked what I was going to tell Jacob when I met him. She'd set up our meeting and her job was done.

"Thanks again for letting me stay during break," I said. "I really had fun. Exploring the city with you was great, and I'll have enough candy for a year after our trip to Dylan's."

Heather smiled. "I had fun too," she said. "But don't expect to stay with me during *every* break or something."

I laughed. "Never."

"And, BTW, I'm going to talk to Julia and Alison about throwing a private back-to-school party in our suite tomorrow night like around seven. It'll be something to look forward to after what you know is going to be a boring, ridic Monday. Want to come?"

"Absolutely," I said. "That sounds like fun. And most def a good idea to have *something* to look forward to tomorrow."

"Cool," Heather said. She gave me a sideways look, waiting for me to say something—probably about my meeting with Jacob.

"See you in class," I said, smiling at her.

Heather and I started down our respective sidewalks and, for a second, I glanced back over my shoulder at her. I half wanted to be following her back to Orchard.

The Trio's suite felt welcoming—there was anxiety about going back to my own room.

But you don't want to avoid the situation with Paige any longer, I told myself. My pace slowed as I walked and I looked around at the campus, trying to distract myself from what I was about to face. I had no idea what I was walking into—whether if Paige would still be as apologetic as she had been—or how I'd react to whatever she said. Paige had tried to reach out to me over break, but I hadn't been ready to talk.

I pulled my pink suitcase behind me and looked at the campus as if I'd been away for more than a week. The leaves were starting to change from green to orange, red, and yellow. The sidewalks were swept clean of even a blade of grass. Students were entering their buildings with suitcases and duffel bags. Soon, the scramble to get ready for class tomorrow would begin.

I reached Winchester Hall and walked up the steps to the door. I grasped the iron railing, pausing for a second and taking a breath.

Just go, I told myself.

I pulled open the door and wheeled my suitcase down the glossy wooden floor of the eighth-grade dorm. Looking at the eggshell white walls, the dry erase board with SUICHIN'S ROOM, and the familiar faint scent of lemon made me feel at home.

I passed door after door until I reached the room I shared with Paige. Our dry erase board had its message in bubbly script that Paige had written in orange marker before we'd left.

HAPPY FALL BREAK! <3, S & P

I couldn't even look at the message. I pushed open the door.

"Hi." Paige, facing the door, stood still and stared at me. Her tone wasn't the Paige I was used to hearing. It wasn't cold or snotty like Heather—it was cautious, unsure.

"Hey," I said. I looked at the neat stacks of clothes on her bed. "When did you get here?"

Paige shrugged. She turned back to her clothes and started putting them on hangers. "I don't know. An hour or so ago, I guess."

I lifted my suitcase onto my bed and unzipped it. Pulling out my clothes, I started unpacking, too, and we were silent as we put away our clothes. The tension in the room was ridiculous. I didn't want things to be like this. Neither Paige nor I needed this extra pressure before school started again. Paige had tried enough to apologize—it was my turn.

"Paige," I said, sitting on the end of my bed. "I'm ready to listen and talk about what happened at the Homecoming dance if you still want to."

Paige smoothed her jean skirt, which looked supercute with black tights, and sat at the edge of her own bed. "I want to talk," she said. "Now that you're ready."

We paused, both looking at each other—seeing who would go first.

I knew it was my turn. "You kept trying to apologize to me after Homecoming," I said. "But you have to understand that I wasn't ready. What you said about me being jealous about you having a boyfriend really, *really* hurt my feelings."

"I told you that I didn't mean what I said," Paige said. "I know it's no excuse for what I said, but I swear that I didn't mean it. I was upset, and I wanted to say something that would hurt you."

"And it did," I said honestly. "Homecoming week was tough on me, and you knew that. It was too much hearing you—of all people—say that to me, after everything I'd gone through all week."

Paige ducked her head. "I know. The entire week was hard on you, and I didn't give you as much support as I should have. *But . . .*"

I sat up a little straighter at that part. "But what?"

"I tried to apologize to you for an entire week," Paige said. "I texted, called . . . and you never wrote me back. Not once. Not even to say you still *weren't* ready to talk. And that night at Butter—you humiliated me in front of Heather."

That made my stomach hurt a little. I had told Paige that I hadn't wanted to talk about our fight in a not-so-private place. "I'm sorry. I should have handled that better. I wish I'd told you that in private instead of saying it like that right there."

Paige's blinked and focused her green eyes on me. "I wish you would have too. That was so unlike you. It was almost like . . . never mind."

"What?" I asked. "You know you can tell me anything."

Paige ran her fingers through her red-gold hair. "It just sounded like something Heather would say, that's all."

Whoa. Considering Paige's dislike for Heather that was a huge insult. I wanted to defend myself and what I'd said, but I didn't want to start another fight with Paige. Not over that comment.

"I was just overwhelmed by seeing you at Butter," I said. "What I said was harsh, and I'm sorry."

I left Heather out of the conversation. She had nothing to do with this—it was between Paige and me.

Paige took a breath and rubbed her hands over her ivory face. "I don't want things to be weird between us. I'm truly sorry for what I said to you, and I didn't mean to hurt your feelings."

"I believe you," I said. "And I'm sorry about Butter. I wish we could have spent the break together. At least there will be plenty more chances for us to do that."

Paige half nodded.

I wanted her to say yes, we did have more opportunities to do that, but she didn't. That stung a little. I shook it off and smiled at Paige.

"So, we're okay?" Paige asked.

I got up, and we hugged. "We're more than okay," I said. "We're best friends and always will be."

That made Paige grin. "I've got so much to tell you about break," she said. "And I want to hear all about yours."

"I want to hear *every* detail about yours, and I'll tell you all about mine, but there's something I have to do first."

Paige gave me the *you better spill* face.

"I'll tell you all about it the second I get back," I said. "Promise."

"You better," Paige said.

I changed out of my wrinkled shirt and pulled on a

cranberry-colored, v-neck, long-sleeve shirt, dark skinny jeans, and black wedges.

"Be back soon," I said to Paige.

I walked out of the room, pulling my phone out of my pocket.

Meet u in an hr? ~S

I sent the text to Jacob.

My phone vibrated seconds later.

Perf. C u there.

Then I headed to the one place that would make me feel comfortable before my meeting with Jacob.

3

ESP

I WALKED TO THE BLACK AND WHITE STABLE, inhaling the scent of clean hay, horses, and sweet grain. Charm's stall was exactly where I needed to be to calm down. Plus, not seeing him for a week was unacceptable!

I hurried past rows of box stalls, ducked around horses in crossties, and sidestepped muck carts.

When I got to Charm's stall, I peered over the door. He was snoozing in the back, one chestnut leg cocked and his head down.

"Hi, gorgeous," I said, my voice soft so I didn't startle him.

Immediately, he lifted his head and turned his ears toward the sound of my voice. I unlatched the stall door and stepped into the sawdust.

When Charm and I reached each other I threw my arms around his neck. I hugged him hard, feeling him lean into me as if he was hugging me back. His coat was spotless and it gleamed like copper. Mike—my favorite groom—had taken perfect care of Charm just like I'd known he would.

I released Charm's neck and stroked his blaze. Kissing his cheek, I squeezed my eyes shut for a second, just happy to be with my horse. Charm looked toward the door and our connectedness, through what I swore was ESP, told me what he was thinking.

"So sorry," I said. "But we're not going for a ride right now. I missed you so much that I wanted to see you. You're also the best listener and I'm about to go do something in a little while that's kind of scary."

Charm's attention left the door, and he looked back at me. I leaned against the stall wall in the back so I could see the door in case anyone approached. The last thing I needed was for someone to overhear my conversation with my horse. Charm turned toward me and nuzzled my ribs, making me laugh.

"Thanks," I said, stroking his neck before grabbing his black leather halter. "I missed you too."

Charm blinked, with what I was sure was understanding,

and pointed his ears at me—like he was telling me to talk.

"It's a looong story," I said. "But over break, Heather hacked into my e-mail account and wrote to Jacob as if she were me."

Charm put back an ear—he still had mixed feelings about Heather.

"At first, I freaked out. I thought I was going to pour a Diet Coke on her or something. I stayed up all night thinking about what she'd done. But even though what she did was wrong—she did what I *didn't* have the guts to do—go after what I want."

I swallowed.

"I want to be with Jacob," I whispered. "I *know* I said I was swearing off boys. And I am! I think. But I have these feelings for Jacob, and I wish there were some way we could be together. I know we can't because it would kill Callie even though they're broken up. I just wish there was some way."

Charm huffed a warm breath into my hand.

"What should I do?" I asked him. "Do I tell Jacob everything I told you? Or do I lie about it and tell him Heather sent the e-mails and I don't agree with anything she said?"

Charm looked at me with beautiful brown eyes and I knew the answer to my question.

"I better go," I said. "I love you so much. *You're* my number one guy. See you tomorrow. You'll *definitely* get your ride."

Charm blinked and if he could smile, I knew he would have.

I kissed his black and pink muzzle, then left the stall. I was ready to face Jacob. It was time to talk.

I walked down the sidewalk, taking a right to the courtyard. That part of the campus was empty since everyone was probably unpacking or catching up with friends after break. I passed the stone benches and walked over the cobblestones.

And there he was. Waiting for me.

Jacob turned, his hands shoved deep in the pocket of his crimson hoodie. I almost couldn't believe that I was staring at him in person after spending most of break imagining him and thinking about what he was doing. His light brown hair and green eyes made it difficult to talk. I semistumbled toward him and stopped, just feet away.

"Hi," I said, my voice so quiet I barely heard it.

"Hey," Jacob said, giving me an easy smile. He gestured toward a bench. "Want to sit?"

"Sure."

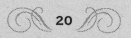

We sat at opposite ends of a bench. I turned to face him, and he looked into my eyes.

"There's no easy way to say this," I said. "So I just have to."

Jacob's lips parted and he looked as if he was trying to prepare himself. As if he was readying himself for me to tell him that I'd thought about it, but wasn't ready to be his girlfriend.

"It's not what you think," I said, immediately wanting to stop the hurt look on his face. "But it is a little complicated."

Jacob looked at me, waiting.

I paused. "I didn't write any of the e-mails. Heather hacked into my e-mail account and told you my phone was broken until the weekend. She was the one writing you."

Jacob's head dropped. "Oh my God," he said. "*Heather* was e-mailing me? I thought it was you the whole time! I had no idea. I feel like such an idiot."

"Wait, please don't," I said. "I was *furious* when I found out what she'd done. I mean, we've sort of become friends and then when I found out . . . I wanted to break her laptop!"

Jacob's face was pink with embarrassment. "*Every* e-mail was from Heather. Every. One." He sighed.

"You don't understand," I said. I had to say it now or I

never would. "Heather . . . told you everything I couldn't."

Jacob looked at me—his green eyes flickering back and forth over my face. "What do you mean?"

"Every e-mail she sent was something I wanted to say to you, but was afraid. I was scared of the drama and what would happen if we started dating. But there's not one thing in those e-mails that I don't feel or mean."

The tinge of pink faded from Jacob's face. He looked at me—his head tilted. "Everything? Even about you wanting to talk about our options about . . . being together?"

"Yes." My voice was a whisper.

Jacob seemed to relax and tense at the same time. He drew a leg under him and looked at me, his gaze intense.

"Before you say anything else, I need to tell you something," he said. "If there's one thing I regret about the entire situation between Callie, you, and me, it's that I let you take the blame for what I did at your party. If I'd done the right thing, I would have told Callie the truth." Jacob dropped his head. "I said nothing and let you lose your best friend. I don't know if I'll ever stop feeling guilty about that."

"You only did it because I asked you to," I said. "I saw

your face that night—you wanted to stand up and tell the truth. But you respected what I wanted enough not to say anything."

Jacob sighed. "I hated every second of you standing there and lying for me."

Instinctively, I scooted closer to him on the bench. "I couldn't let her or anyone else think awful things about you. I care about you, Jacob, and it was easier for me to have everyone hate me than to have them be mad at you."

Jacob's eyes stayed on mine. "Do you know how amazing you are?"

I blushed. "Yeah, so amazing that I'm here and wanting to talk about . . ." I let my sentence trail off.

Jacob didn't press me to finish my sentence—he just waited.

"I want to talk about the possibility of us trying again. And after all I put you through—after I kept saying no, I would understand if you didn't want to."

Jacob reached over and slipped his hand into mine. "You have no idea how long I've been hoping you'd say that."

I smiled—and felt the same way I had when I'd first looked at him—those clichéd butterflies, the sweaty palms, and a heartbeat I couldn't calm.

"We never had a chance," he said. "Too many things went wrong so early."

"I know. But I don't know how to do this! I want this—I really do. I just don't know how I'd handle Callie and everyone looking at us and hating us. This sounds so selfish, but I want to work out things with us *and* have a drama-free semester."

Jacob placed his hand on top of mine. "We're going to figure it out and I *promise* you'll have a drama-free semester."

"How?"

He looked down, then back at me. "We'll talk more this week. I know we can do this. And to start things right, on Friday, after the stress of the first week is over, I'm telling Callie the truth. She has to know what happened at your birthday party."

"Jacob, no. No, no, no," I said, my voice rising. "You can't tell her the truth—I don't want you to. We'll come up with another way—something—to handle this."

He shook his head. "I have to, Sasha. I've been making this huge mistake the whole time, and I've got to make things right. You'll have a chance at getting your best friend back."

He got up, his eyes never leaving me. "I want to prove

to you that I care about you as much as I've been saying I do. And this is the best way to do that—I'm going to show you."

And with that, he gave me a soft smile. It left me staring after him as he left the courtyard.

4

ONE OF *THOSE* GIRLS

I REACHED THE STABLE WELL BEFORE MONDAY morning's riding team meeting. We had a meeting and lesson this morning to kick off our week of preparation for the schooling show on Sunday. Mr. Conner, my riding instructor, had e-mailed everyone last night to let us know to tack up our horses and meet him in the indoor arena.

All morning, Paige and I had chatted sporadically as we'd gotten dressed. She didn't have to leave as early as I did, so she'd stayed behind in our room. Things weren't bad between us, but they weren't . . . *right* yet either. Maybe it was going to take time after our blowup at the Homecoming dance for things to be okay between us. But I wasn't worried about my friendship with Paige. We'd bonded since the first night I'd been at Canterwood. I knew we'd get our full friendship back.

I thought back to our talk last night about break. I'd told her everything about how Heather had e-mailed Jacob as me. Paige had been furious. She'd asked how I'd made it through the ride back to school with Heather. I'd told her that I understood why Heather had e-mailed Jacob, even though I hated her methods. When the conversation had ended, I could tell Paige wanted to ask me the big question—if I wanted to get back with Jacob now that I wasn't with Eric. But she hadn't and I was relieved since I wasn't sure if I would have been ready to talk about it yet.

I walked down the stable aisle, my boot heels thudding on the concrete as I went to the tack room. Rows of gleaming saddles straddled racks and bridles hung from golden hooks.

I grabbed Charm's black saddle, bridle, and saddle pad, carefully balancing everything as I walked to his stall. Charm was probably still sleeping—he liked to snooze as late as he could.

I put his tack down on the trunk outside his stall and called to him, looking inside the box stall. "Charm?" Just like I'd predicted—he was sleeping in the back corner with his head down. He lifted his head, looking up at me and blinking.

"Time to wake up, sleepy," I said. "We'll get you all nice and shiny and go to our lesson."

Charm's eyes looked a little less glazed over at the mention of grooming. He loved any attention and being brushed was one of his favorite things.

I held his halter, leading him out of his stall and into the aisle. The pair of crossties in front of his stall was empty, and I clipped the ties to the side of his halter. He lifted his head, watching the activity around him. Other riders started to arrive—I saw Heather had crosstied Aristocrat a few stalls ahead of us.

Heather leaned down to rifle through Aristocrat's tack trunk. She stood, saw me, and waved.

"Hey," I mouthed, waving back.

We both got to work—there was never time to talk before morning lessons. I grabbed the dandy brush from Charm's tack box and ran it over his withers, back, and legs. Dust whisked off his hindquarters and flew into the air.

"How *do* you get so dirty overnight?" I teased. "Aren't you supposed to be sleeping?"

Charm huffed, turning his head to look at me with a look as if he wanted to roll his eyes.

I patted his shoulder. "Kidding, kidding," I said.

I took the softer body brush and took my time going over his neck, chest, and barrel. The brush made his coat shine.

After I picked his hooves I combed his mane and tail and cleaned his nostrils and eyes with a wipe. Then it was time to tack him up.

He was awake now and all about getting to our lesson. He'd been away from the arena for a week, so he was probably ready to stretch his legs. Charm didn't move as I smoothed the saddle pad onto his back, placed the English saddle on top, and tightened the girth.

As I tightened it I shook my head at the memory of our early days together. My parents had bought Charm for me when he was five and I was a fairly new rider. Supersmart Charm had taken advantage of me whenever he could. One of his first tricks after I'd taken him home was blowing out his stomach when I was tightening his girth. Then, he'd breathed normally when I put my foot in the stirrup to mount. The saddle had slipped sideways, and I'd ended up on the ground.

Not cool.

But he hadn't done that in years.

I finished tightening his girth and picked up his bridle,

slinging it over my shoulder. It took me seconds to unclip the crossties. I put the reins over Charm's head and left them looped around his neck. I placed the bit on my palm—holding the crown piece of the bridle. Charm took the bit without hesitation. The crown piece settled over his bridle path.

"Time for a trim soon," I said. Charm would need to be clipped and bathed before the schooling show on Sunday.

I took my helmet out of the trunk and snapped it on. I looked down at my fawn-colored breeches and royal purple shirt, checking for any bits of hay or dirt from grooming Charm. It was my first lesson in a week; I wanted to look ready.

"Let's go," I said to Charm, patting his neck.

Ahead of us Heather had already led Aristocrat away. Charm kept his head by my shoulder as we walked down the middle of the mostly empty aisle. The only riders here who had a lesson with Mr. Conner right now were Heather and I, since we were the only two middle school students at Canterwood on the Youth Equestrian National Team. The YENT allowed Mr. Conner to teach our lessons, but he had to report often to Mr. Nicholson, the head scout for the YENT. It was a team that Callie, Julia, and Alison all wanted to make—a decision that would be made at the next team tryout.

I stopped in midstep thinking about Julia and Alison. They'd been kicked off the advanced riding team and forced to miss YENT tryouts because of Jasmine. The former Canterwood student had framed them for cheating. With my help, the girls had proven their innocence and were prepping for the next chance at the YENT.

And Callie . . . I closed my eyes, thinking about my former best friend. She'd tried out for the YENT and hadn't made it. More than anything, I wanted her to make the team this time—it was her dream.

Stop thinking about that now, I told myself. *You've got to focus and show Mr. Conner that you worked hard over break.*

I started forward again, and Charm followed me into the arena. We stopped beside Heather and Aristocrat. The darker chestnut Thoroughbred laid back his ears a fraction as Charm approached. The two horses had never gotten along and were in constant competition with each other—just like Heather and I had been.

"Back to lessons at this evil hour," Heather said with a wry smile.

"No kidding. But I did miss it. Just not the getting up early part."

"Me too."

Heather looked at me and the look on her face told me what she was going to ask.

"How'd things with Jacob go?" Heather asked.

My blush must have given her my answer.

Heather grinned. "Sooo . . . you two *are* getting back together? I mean, I'm just assuming from your red face and grin that you're barely able to hide."

I shoved her arm. "Stop! We had a great chat, and we're going to keep talking this week. We both decided we want to try."

Heather's eyes flickered over my face. "But what?"

Thinking about this part made my stomach hurt. "He's going to tell Callie the truth on Friday," I said. "He said he made a mistake this entire time by letting me take the blame and he wants to prove to me that he cares enough by talking to Callie."

Heather nodded. "He's giving you a chance to get your friend back. You have to let him go with his gut. If Jacob wants to do that for you, then let him. It's obviously still weighing on him."

"I know it is. But—"

I stopped midsentence when Mr. Conner walked through the entrance with a girl I'd never seen before. Her long black hair was in a side braid and her bangs came down just over her eyebrows. She led a tall gray gelding that looked to be part Andalusian with a thick mane and wavy tail. She smiled at us, her brown almond-shaped eyes warm.

"Hi, girls," Mr. Conner said, addressing Heather and me. He stopped and the new girl stopped beside him.

"Hi," we said back.

As we greeted her, I noticed her clothes. Tall, shiny black boots, breeches that looked as if they'd never been worn, and a soft pink v-neck shirt that looked like something I'd wear on a date.

"Heather, Sasha," Mr. Conner said. "I'd like to introduce you to Brit Chan and her horse Apollo. Brit's a new transfer to Canterwood."

"Hey," I said, smiling at her. I remembered what it felt like to be the new girl.

"Hi," Heather said. Her tone was a little less friendly than mine.

"Brit rode for the YENT at her old school," Mr. Conner said. "She was selected during the same round of tryouts as both of you."

Heather stiffened slightly. I knew Heather. She was no longer looking at Brit as another girl at school—Heather now saw Brit as competition. As a rider who was on *our* YENT team.

"Mr. Conner," Heather said. "If Brit is on the YENT now, what about Julia, Alison, and Callie? They're all working for the next tryout."

Mr. Conner nodded at Heather, as if he'd expected this question from her. "Because Brit came to us as a YENT rider, there will still be an open slot on our team for another Canterwood student."

That answer seemed to make Heather relax a little. I went back to looking at Brit. She stood there—so calm and seemingly not intimidated by her new teammates. There was something about her that I hadn't seen before in any student at Canterwood. I couldn't figure out just what "it" was, but when I looked at Brit, I wanted to talk to her more.

"Please go ahead and mount your horses and we'll get started with the lesson," Mr. Conner said.

I gathered the reins, slipped my toe into the stirrup iron, and swung my other leg over the back of the saddle. Heather eased Aristocrat next to Brit's horse. I cringed, sure Heather was going to say something snarky to her.

"Nice shirt," Heather said. "Fall Prada collection."

Brit nodded. "Yeah, thanks."

And I'd just liked it because of the color. Was Brit one of *those* girls? A girl who'd be BFFs with the most popular girls in two seconds? What if . . . *no.* Not going there. I'd been around the girl for all of five seconds and I was already worrying that she was the new Jasmine on campus. *Stop judging her and ride already,* I told myself.

Heather rode Aristocrat away from Brit and toward the wall. Brit and her horse ended up between Charm and Aristocrat. We started the horses at a walk near the wall. Charm and I were behind Brit—I watched as she moved Apollo around at a relaxed walk.

"Trot," Mr. Conner called.

Within strides, we'd all let our horses out at a trot and we were posting. Brit moved ever so slightly in the saddle—her arms tucked against her sides and her heels down.

I'd only seen her at a trot, but I had a feeling the more I'd see of her riding, the clearer it would become why she'd made the YENT.

"Reverse direction and keep trotting," Mr. Conner said.

We crossed over the center of the arena and I sat for a beat to post on the correct diagonal.

Now, I was in front of Brit and Heather was behind

her. It made me a little nervous to have Brit watch me ride, but I tried to think of it like any other class and pretend Heather was the only one in the arena with Charm and me.

Mr. Conner stood in the center of the dirt arena, his glance switching from us to the clipboard in his hands that he used to take notes. He ran a hand over his short black hair, his dark brown eyes intense on us. He wore his usual hunter green Canterwood Crest Academy polo shirt with CCA stitched in gold thread under the collar. Canterwood was big on school spirit and the school colors were everywhere on campus.

I looked between Charm's pointed ears and wondered how Brit felt about her first lesson here. I'd been terrified during my first class. But from what I'd seen so far, she appeared to be cool.

"Sasha," Mr. Conner said. "Lower your hands and keep them still."

I eased my hands down a couple of inches and held them steady. *You've got to work on that,* I scolded myself. For the next few strides, I concentrated on my hands and made sure they stayed still and in the right position. The sound of hoofbeats on the arena dirt was almost like a tune I wished I could capture and put on my iPod. The rhythmic sound pulsed into my brain, relaxing my body. I didn't have to concentrate on keeping the correct position—it was right without me thinking about it.

"Ease them into a canter, please," Mr. Conner said.

I squeezed my legs against Charm's sides and gave him rein. He moved from a trot into a smooth canter. His Thoroughbred/Belgian blood helped him take long strides, and we were almost halfway around the arena before I realized it.

"Change direction," Mr. Conner said. "And Heather, your legs keep creeping too far forward."

We kept our horses at a steady canter as we switched direction. Again, I was behind Brit. At a canter, I was *really* able to see her in action. She rocked to Apollo's easy strides, and I *knew* Brit had to have trained at a fantastic school. She'd probably tell us all about it the second we got off our horses.

"Brit," Mr. Conner said. "Watch your back position. You're hunching forward too much."

In front of me, Brit straightened. Mr. Conner kept us cantering the horses around the arena for two more laps. It felt so good to be back in *my* arena. It had been fun riding at Heather's old stable during break, but this was where I was most comfortable.

Mr. Conner raised his hand. "Pull them to a walk," he said.

Heather, Brit, and I slowed the horses. I ran a hand down Charm's neck. He was warm, but not even close to sweating. Mr. Conner's lessons kept him well-conditioned. The exercise hadn't fazed him.

"We're going to stick to flatwork this morning," Mr. Conner said. "We have plenty of time before the schooling show to work on jumping. Brit will be joining us at the show, so we'll all be working together to get ready."

This girl wowed me. It was her first week here *and* she was showing on Sunday.

Mr. Conner walked out of the center of the arena, standing off to the side. "Start your horses in large circles at a sitting trot," he said. "After each rotation, make the circle smaller. Before you feel your horse start to strain, stop."

Charm and I definitely needed practice with circles, especially on his left side. He was stiff sometimes and the circles helped him stretch and flex.

I asked Charm to trot and guided him in a large circle. Brit was in the middle of the arena with Heather off to the side. I didn't let myself focus on Brit or Heather—I had to keep my attention on Charm. We had to get the most of every second of the lesson. Especially with the schooling show so close.

Charm's muscles felt loose as we completed our first rotation. I pulled the reins in slightly, guiding him into a circle that was a fraction smaller. As we turned toward the center of the arena, I noted the intensity on Brit's face and how her gelding seemed so in tune with her. Heather and Aristocrat were also completing a circle that showed off the beautiful Thoroughbred's movements.

I tightened the reins a notch and Charm's circle got smaller. Beneath me, I felt him start to lean a little to the side, but still keep his balance. He'd usually begin to have to work harder to keep a steady pace and even footing after a few more laps. I took him around twice more before I could sense the strain through his back. I let him into a big circle, then changed directions.

Charm moved much easier this way. He made two more rotations in this direction than he had in the previous.

Mr. Conner made us do a few more circles, then spirals, before raising his hand and signaling us to move our horses in front of him.

"Great start," he said. He looked over to Brit. "I hope that you'll feel more comfortable with each lesson. Please don't hesitate to come to me or any of my riders if you have questions."

"Thank you," Brit said.

"Have a good day back at class and see you at our next lesson," Mr. Conner said.

Heather, Brit, and I dismounted and Brit followed Heather and me out of the arena and into the aisle.

Mike and Doug, the other stable groom, met us and smiled.

"We take care of the horses in the morning," Mike said to Brit. "Your guy is all yours in the afternoon."

"Thanks so much," Brit said. She handed her horse's reins to Mike, and Doug took Charm and Aristocrat. We unsnapped our helmets, starting toward the tack room.

"What'd you think?" I asked Brit.

"Mr. Conner seems like a great instructor," Brit said. "I know I'm going to learn a lot from him."

"You definitely will," I said. We entered the tack room and found Julia and Alison inside, dressed in yoga pants and hoodies.

"What're you guys doing here?" Heather asked.

"We heard there was a new transfer onto the YENT team," Alison said. Her long sandy-brown hair was wavy and loose around her shoulders.

"Yeah," Julia said. "We wanted to catch some of your lesson, but we overslept."

Both girls didn't even look at Brit—they acted as if she was a regular, even though Canterwood was a fairly small campus.

"Hi," Brit said, stepping forward. She smiled at Julia and Alison. "I'm the new student, Brit."

Julia ran a hand through her short blond bob, her eyes widening when she looked at Brit.

"Oh," she said, an edge to her voice. "So *you're* the YENT transfer?"

"She just said that," Heather interrupted. "We need to get back to Orchard before we're late for class."

"Orchard?" Brit asked, smiling. "That's where I live."

"Walk back with us, then," Heather said. She turned to me. "Later, Silver."

Heather ignored the shocked glances from Julia and Alison and motioned for Brit to follow her. Brit flashed a smile at me.

"Nice to meet you, Sasha," she said. "Maybe I'll see you in class."

"That would be cool. See you around," I said.

Heather, Julia, Alison, and Brit left the tack room with me staring after them.

5

SMALL-TOWN GIRL

BACK IN MY ROOM, I HURRIED TO SHOWER, dress and get to class. Paige had already left—a star-shaped sticky note on my bed said she'd had a meeting with Ms. Utz, our guidance counselor, this morning.

The morning's classes weren't any different from the classes before break. I'd had a fantasy that the teachers would suddenly become easier on us and would assign no or little homework on the first day.

So. Wrong.

By the time I got to math, my assignment notebook was full of so many things that I'd be up way after lights out.

I walked into math class and took my usual seat, opening the fifty-pound hardback textbook and trying to remember the formulas I was supposed to have memorized over break. Callie was in this class, too, so I always kept my gaze on the whiteboard or my desk.

"Is anyone sitting here?"

I looked up and saw Brit gesturing to the desk across from me.

"Nope," I said. "That's what's cool about this class. We can sit wherever we want."

"Cool," Brit said. "None of my teachers at my old school ever did that."

I started to ask Brit where she'd gone to school, but my attention was caught by a purple notebook covered in glittery star stickers.

"Those are so cute," I said. "I love stickers." I closed the cover of my own notebook, showing her the horse and heart stickers that covered mine.

Brit leaned over, pointing to a sticker of a chestnut horse head. "That looks like your horse. What's his name?"

"Charm," I said. "He's a sweet horse. I'll have to introduce you two at our next lesson."

Brit grinned. "I'd love that."

We smiled at each other. "So, where did you—"

I stopped talking when Ms. Utz, who also taught math,

walked in with Callie close behind. Callie slid into a seat near the door, not even looking in my direction.

"Welcome back, class," Ms. Utz said. "Let's take attendance and get right to work. I know you've all missed math over break."

The entire class looked around at each other. That was *so* untrue. For me, anyway.

I tried to pay attention, but my mind kept wandering to Brit. I'd been just about to ask her where she'd transferred from. She had the look of a girl who'd come from a fancy school like Heather, but there was something different about the way she acted. All of the seats filled around her, as if everyone wanted to get to know the new girl.

Out of the corner of my eye, I looked at her clothes. Dark blue skinny jeans tucked into black boots with a slight heel. Her dark brown three-quarters sleeve shirt had buttons down the front with a few ruffles. She looked like definite Trio material. But there was something about her that wasn't quite Trio-like.

Forty minutes later, Brit and I walked out of class together, long after Callie had disappeared from the classroom. We matched strides and walked out of the math building. As we walked down the hallway, everyone smiled at her and they looked as if they wished they could join us.

"What class do you have next?" I asked Brit.

She pulled her schedule out of her bag and scanned it. "I have a meeting with the guidance counselor's assistant," she said. "Then lunch."

"I have lunch now," I said. "The cafeteria is halfway to the admissions building. I can walk you toward there, if you want."

"That'd be great," Brit said, flipping her braid behind her shoulder.

We walked down the sidewalk, dodging other students who were rushing to class, and I enjoyed the light breeze and sun on my face.

"I was about to ask before Ms. Utz came in," I said. "Where did you transfer from?"

"Charles Middle School," Brit said.

"That's twenty minutes from where I went to school!" I said. "I'm from Union."

"No way! Omigod, that's so cool," Brit said, bouncing. "I thought everyone here would be from New York City or some other big place."

"Not me. Small-town girl all the way."

Brit smiled. "This is too awesome. Where did you ride?"

"Briar Creek Stable," I said. "What about you?"

"Pemberton. I've heard of Briar Creek. We probably competed against each other at a local show and didn't even know it."

"Probably." It felt crazy to meet someone else who was from a small town. Brit was from a city that wasn't much bigger than Union, but she'd walked onto campus as if she'd moved here from New York or Los Angeles.

"I was sure you'd transferred from a private school," I said. "Where did you go to ride in Charles?"

"My mom drove me an hour each way to Pemberton Stables," Brit said. She shifted her backpack. "She probably spent more time in the car taking me to lessons or waiting for me than she did at home."

Her tone was joking, but I could tell she was serious.

"I couldn't imagine two hours in the car to get to the stable," I said. "How often did you go?"

"Every day," Brit said. "I had to, if I wanted to make the YENT."

We rounded the sidewalk and I reached the entrance to the cafeteria. If someone hadn't laughed loud enough to jostle me out of our conversation, I would have missed my stop and kept talking to her. It felt so good to talk to someone else who *got* it.

"The guidance office," I said. "Is in the building straight ahead."

"Thanks for walking with me," Brit said. "It's so great to meet someone."

"No prob," I said. "Bye."

Brit and I both walked away smiling. When I turned to look to see if she'd gone in the right direction, I saw a group of eighth-grade guys staring at her and whispering. They were all smiling, and they didn't stop watching her until she went inside.

While I waited for the lunch lady to serve my mac and cheese and ham sandwich, I kept going over our conversation in my head. Brit hadn't tried to hide where she was from—she was proud of being from Charles. And I had a feeling that once everyone—Heather included—found out where she was from, she would still be supercool Brit Chan.

6

I'M NEVER WRONG

I *FINALLY* GOT BACK TO MY ROOM AFTER class, tossed my backpack onto the floor and fell backward onto my bed. Paige, right behind me, mirrored my collapse.

"This was the most intense Monday *ever*," I said.

"No kidding," Paige said, rubbing her eyes. "There's no way I'll finish even half my homework before tomorrow. I'll have to get up at, like, five to get it all done."

"Same," I said. "I've got a zillion things to do, and I have no clue where to start."

My phone buzzed on my lamp table, and I swiped it. *Come ovr @ 7.—H*

I sat up, realizing I'd forgotten about Heather's back-to-school get-together tonight and really needed to get my homework done. Like, right now.

I spread my books on my bed, opening my notebook.

"Wow," Paige said. "I was going to take a breather since we just got back from class, but you're making me feel so guilty."

"I have to start now," I said. "I forgot that Heather invited me to the Trio's suite tonight for a back-to-school thing."

Paige paused, playing with the ends of her hair.

"Oh. I didn't know you were going there. Yeah, then. You better get started now."

Tension crept back into the room—something I didn't want.

"I can totally blow them off," I said. "We could do our homework together and chill."

"No, go," Paige said. She smiled a genuine Paige smile. "I was actually going to text Geena or someone and see if she wanted to go over notes from our cooking class. We have a new recipe due on Friday."

"Oh, cool," I said. "But I'm still your honorary taste tester, right?"

Paige nodded. "Always."

And with that we started our homework. I worked until sixty-thirty and then stopped, wanting time to get ready and make it to the Trio's suite on time. Heather would probably lock me out of their room if I was even a minute late.

While Paige kept working I re-straightened my hair and applied fresh powder and blush. I scanned my lipgloss case, looking for the perfect shade before settling on a Lip Smackers wild raspberry. I didn't want to overdo it for a night in.

I exited the bathroom, grabbing my purse and phone. "I'm going," I said to Paige. "Did you ever get in touch with Geena?"

"Um, yeah," Paige said. "She'll be here any minute."

"Have fun!"

"You too," Paige said as I left our room.

I walked down Winchester's hallway and paused in the doorway of our dorm monitor, Livvie.

"Hey," I said, peeking my head in. "It's okay if I go to Heather's for a while, right?"

Livvie looked up from her desk where she was typing on her laptop. She checked the clock on the wall. "Sure. Just be back by nine."

"Sure thing," I said. "Thanks."

I left and walked across the streetlamp-lit campus to Orchard dorm. The old-fashioned lanterns cast a soft yellow glow.

Callie lived in Orchard, too, and I crossed my fingers that I'd make it to the Trio's suite without seeing her.

I pulled open the door and walked down the hallway. With its cranberry-colored walls, dark carpeting and ornate lighting—Orchard was one of my favorite dorms. I loved visiting and felt more and more comfortable every time I came to the Trio's suite.

I reached their door and knocked lightly on the dark wood.

A frowning Julia pulled open the door and ushered me inside without a word.

"You okay?" I asked, knowing she probably wouldn't tell me.

"Oh, fine," Julia grumbled. "Totally fine. *They're* all in the common room getting snacks."

"You mean Heather and Alison?" I asked as I kicked off my shoes and walked to the couch, sitting on the far end from Julia.

Julia flopped into the oversize recliner and rolled her eyes. "No. Heather, Alison, and *Brit.* Apparently, she's coming tonight."

"You don't like her?" I asked.

Julia folded her arms. "She's fine. Whatever. But did

we really need to invite someone else into the Trio now? Especially some new girl we don't even know?"

"Who asked her to come?"

"Alison," Julia said. "And Heather was like, 'That's totally cool.'"

"It's just for one back-to-school casual thing," I said. "She's not going to invite her into the Trio."

Before Julia could respond, the door opened and Heather, Alison, and Brit walked inside. All three girls were laughing.

"What's so funny?" Julia asked in a flat voice.

"Omigod," Alison said, taking a deep breath. "Brit just told us the funniest story about her cute neighbor at home."

"Hey, guys," Brit said to Julia and me.

"Hi," I said back.

Julia's arms seemed to tighten across her chest. Heather, Alison, and Brit put the snacks and drinks they were carrying on the table. They had a spread of cheese, crackers, and pepperoni and then more casual snacks like Fritos and chips and salsa.

"Brit, sit wherever you want," Heather said.

"Cool, thanks."

Brit sat beside me on the couch. She glanced around the Trio's suite. "This place is awesome. I love it!"

"We got lucky to get a suite," Alison said, taking the

other recliner. "We wouldn't be the Trio if we were split up again like last year."

Julia let out a barely audible *huff*. "We're not the *Trio* right now. It's like we're letting anyone in these days."

Heather put a glass on the table with more force than necessary and glared at Julia. "You need to chill."

Julia's face reddened.

Brit shifted on the couch. "If this was a private party and I'm crashing, I'll totally go," she said.

"Don't be silly," Heather said. She sat next to Brit on the couch. "We *invited* you. There's no problem." The last sentence was directed at Julia.

"Okay," Brit said. She smiled at Heather. Julia managed to pull her mouth into a half smile that looked more like a snarl. Heather turned on the TV and started the movie. We all began snacking and watching the new comedy. The movie was a good release from the pressure of Canterwood on a Monday and soon we were all laughing—even Julia. As I watched the movie with the Trio and Brit, I couldn't help but think how right this felt and how much I wanted to be here.

An hour and a half later, I stretched as the credits rolled. I had orange Cheetos dust on my fingers, and I tried to scrub it off with a napkin.

"Thanks for having me over," I said. "It was fun. Definitely the perfect way to end a Monday."

"It *so* was," Brit said. She got up off the couch and started gathering plastic cups and paper plates. "Thanks, for inviting me too. Everyone's been so welcoming."

"Sit with us at lunch tomorrow," Heather said.

"That'd be great," Brit said. She grinned at Heather as she followed Alison into the kitchenette to throw away our trash.

"We need to keep her close," Heather said, her voice low so Brit and Alison didn't hear.

"Why?" Julia hissed. "She's a new girl. So what?"

Heather shot Julia a look that made the blond girl shrink into her recliner. "Because A: We *want* her in our group. And B: I'm never wrong. We'll discuss this later."

Brit and Alison walked back to us, and Heather flashed a smile at the new girl. "It was fun hanging out." Heather looked at Brit and me. "See you later."

Brit and I put on our shoes and waved good-bye. We walked down the hallway, and Brit, looking at me, grinned. "That was fun. I really like them."

"Yeah," I said. "We had a rocky start, but they're all cool girls."

"Oooh," Brit said. "Sounds like a story for another night."

I laughed. "Deal. We can go to the Sweet Shoppe sometime and chat."

"This is my room," Brit said, pointing to a door that had yet to be decorated.

"Isn't that one of the doubles?" I asked.

Brit nodded and pulled keys out of her pocket. There was a sparkly "B" keychain with rhinestones. "I transferred so late that there wasn't space for me to move in with someone else. So, I got a double to myself until I get a roommate."

"That's so awesome to have your own space," I said. "It's probably nice to have time to yourself while you're still adjusting to things."

Brit played with her keys. "It is, but I like being around other people. I'm kind of hoping that someone transfers soon." She smiled.

"Sure," I said. "I get that side of it too. I've got to get back to my room, but see you in class."

Brit and I went our separate ways, and as I walked back to my dorm, I couldn't stop thinking about how interesting she was and how Julia had such a strong reaction to her. She *seriously* couldn't think Brit was a threat to her spot in the Trio or that Heather would ever add another girl to their clique. No matter how friendly I became with all or any of them, I'd always be on the outside. And that wasn't necessarily a bad thing—I wasn't sure, even if they'd asked, if being part of their group was what I wanted. Right now, hanging out with them was fun. Heather had been great support over the past couple of weeks.

But I also missed Paige, and I was ready to chill with her for a while.

7

IT WAS
MY CHOICE

"HEY, ROOMIE," I CALLED DOWN THE WINCHESTER
hallway. Paige was unlocking our door. She jumped, drop-
ping her keys.

"Geez! You scared me, Sasha!" Paige said. She picked
up her keys, shoving them into the lock.

"Sorry," I said. "I didn't mean to."

We walked inside our room and put down our purses.
I sat in the middle of my bed, feeling bad for scaring her.

"You didn't have to apologize," Paige said, pulling her
hair into a ponytail. "I had way too much caffeine today,
and I totally overreacted."

"Don't worry about it," I said. "You know how I am
on too much Diet Coke. I'm totally hyper and I drive you
crazy until I crash."

That made Paige grin. "How was hanging out with the Trio?"

"Awesome," I said. "Alison invited Brit—this new girl in Orchard—to watch the movie with us, and it was lots of fun. She's on the YENT too."

Paige sat cross-legged on her bed so we could face each other. "I heard there was a new transfer, but I haven't met her yet. She's not in any of my classes."

"You'd really like her," I said. "She's in a class with me, and we got to talk a little. I found out she's from a small town too—really close to mine. And you'd never guess it by the way she acts and how people here treat her."

"What do you mean?" Paige asked.

"Like how the Trio mocked me for months for being from Union. They don't do that to Brit. She's just like them in the way she dresses and has that . . . confidence, I guess, but she's not mean or snarky like they are."

"She sounds really cool," Paige said. I noticed a hint of distraction in her voice. "You'll have to introduce me to her sometime."

"I will," I said. "So, let's talk about you for a sec. Did you end up meeting Geena and working on a new recipe?"

"Yeah," Paige said. "We met up in our common room."

"Did you guys come up with something amazing?" I

asked, thinking about the tasty dishes Paige had created in the past. "Like, cake? Or brownies? Or another dessert that I have to try the second you make it?"

Paige got off the bed and started packing her bag for classes tomorrow. "We were *supposed* to work on the recipe, but Geena got a text from her roommate and she had to leave early."

"So Paige Parker took over the Winchester common room and came up with something on her own, didn't she?" I asked in a teasing voice. "Tell me. What is it, and, most important, *where* is it?"

Paige shoved her math book into her backpack. "Actually, I left when Geena did. I went to the Sweet Shoppe."

I got up off my bed and walked to my desk, closing books and notebooks. "Oh, cool. Get anything good?"

"Iced pomegranate lemonade," Paige said. "It was awesome."

"Yum. Maybe you and Geena can make a dessert with pomegranates or something."

Paige nodded as she walked toward the bathroom. "Yeah, that's a good idea. I'm going to shower and go to bed. I'm really, really tired after the first day back."

"Me too," I said.

Paige shut the door behind her, and I stared at it for a few seconds. She wasn't mad that I'd gone to the Trio's, was she? She knew Heather and I had become friends after I'd spent break with her. Plus, Paige had other friends too, and I'd never cared if she wanted to hang out with them. The situation with them *was* a little different, but as my best friend, Paige had to understand that it was my choice to hang out with Heather, Julia, and Alison and she needed to support me.

I went over to my closet and busied myself with picking out my clothes for tomorrow—a welcome distraction from whatever was going on with Paige. And if she kept being weird about me hanging out with the Trio, I'd talk to her. But tonight, I didn't want to let go of my good mood from hanging out in Orchard.

8

THERE'S ALWAYS
ANOTHER SEAT OPEN

THE NEXT MORNING, PAIGE WAS BACK TO HER
bubbly, cheerful self. There wasn't a hint of weirdness
from last night, and Paige chatted about classes and meeting Geena later. I was relieved that she seemed cool now.

I started to reach for my phone to put it in my pocket
when it buzzed. Flipping it open, I smiled at what I read.

Just saying hi. Hope 2 run into u 2day.

Jacob.

I closed my phone before Paige could see the message.

"Heather," I said to Paige, feeling the need to say
something. Paige was zipping up her peep toe ankle boot.
"Our lesson is outside today. Hopefully jumping."

"That's your fave, so cool," Paige said, smiling.

I felt a twinge in my stomach about hiding the text,

but I wasn't ready to tell her about Jacob yet. I'd sworn to Paige that I was taking a break from boys to focus on riding and school. Paige had no idea that Jacob and I had decided to get back together.

"Ready?" Paige asked. She shouldered her bag.

"Ready."

We left the dorm and I blinked as we stepped into the bright sunshine. The campus was busy as students hurried to classes. Paige and I walked down the sidewalk. We'd gotten up early enough this morning to make it to breakfast. But I was going solo. Paige had to meet Geena at Orchard to swap recipes before their class.

"See you in English," I said when we reached the split in the sidewalk.

"Bye," Paige said.

I got to the caf and piled three blueberry pancakes on my plate. I picked a small vacant table near the window and sat down. Once my pancakes were smeared with butter and syrup, I jammed a giant bite into my mouth.

"Mind if I sit here?"

I looked up and Brit stood in front of me, holding her breakfast tray.

"Sit," I said, my mouth too full to say anything else.

I couldn't believe she was sitting next to *me*. She could

have sat anywhere—even with the Trio—but she'd chosen to sit with me. I felt curious eyes on us as everyone watched the too-cool-to-mess-with new girl sit with the former newbie-from-a-hick-town.

"Those pancakes look great," Brit said. "I love blueberries."

I glanced at her plate. She'd gotten pancakes too—banana.

"The banana pancakes are just as good here," I said. "I'd recommend anything but the meatloaf. It's just . . . scary."

Brit laughed. "Noted. No Canterwood meatloaf."

"How are you doing so far?" I asked. "It can be so overwhelming."

Brit cut into her pancakes. "I'm doing okay. Still getting used to my schedule and the new curriculum, but otherwise, I feel like I belong here."

"That's great. You definitely seem to fit in with everyone." I looked over at the people who were still staring at us. "It looks like everyone wanted you to sit with them."

Brit lifted her head, glancing around casually. "Oh, please," she said, laughing. "No one even knows me."

It was my turn to laugh. "Doesn't matter. You walked

into school like you owned the place and if you haven't noticed—everyone wants to be your friend. The guys at the stable are totally into you, BTW."

"What? No!" Brit's cheeks turned pink.

"I was outside the tack room and I heard them talking about how hot the new girl was," I said. "They think you're supertalented. You'll probably have a boyfriend by the end of the week."

Brit took a bite of pancake. "No thanks. I think I'll wait till I've been here long enough to *not* get lost on campus before I have a boyfriend."

We smiled at each other and went back to our breakfasts. Earlier, I'd been upset that Paige hadn't been able to make breakfast, but now I was glad I'd had the time to get to know Brit better.

After we finished, Brit and I left the caf together.

"Sasha!"

I looked away from Brit and saw Paige walking up another sidewalk toward us.

"Hey," I said.

Paige reached us, and Brit and I stopped.

"Paige," I said. "This is Brit. Brit, this is my roommate."

"Hey," Paige said, flashing a smile. "Nice to meet you."

"Hi. It's cool to finally meet Sasha's roommate," Brit

said. She brushed her bangs out of her eyes and pointed to Paige's boots. "Those are supercute. I love them."

"Thanks," Paige said.

I looked at them and noted how they had a similar style of dress. Brit was in knee-high black boots and a green silk shirt. Silver hoops flashed in the sunlight and the outfit plus accessories was so something Paige would wear.

"I've got to get to class, but see you!" Brit said.

"Bye," Paige and I said.

We split up from Brit and kept walking to English.

"She's nice, right?" I asked.

"Definitely," Paige said. "She seems cool."

We reached the English building and took the stairs to Mr. Davidson's classroom. The advanced English class only had ten students, including Alison, and I loved how we got to sit in a circle and talk about whatever book we were reading. But Mr. Davidson was strict about participation—if you couldn't answer questions about the past night's reading, you had to leave class with a zero for the day.

I took my usual seat next to Paige, and we pulled out our copies of *The Secret Garden* and the notebooks with notes we'd taken over break. Alison, pulling her hair over to one side as she walked, sat down beside me.

"Hey, guys," she said. "Paige, how was your break?"

Alison and Paige had bonded during Homecoming—they'd both been obsessed about it.

"It was fun," Paige said. Blinking, I realized that Paige and I hadn't talked much about her break.

At. All.

I didn't even know what she'd done during the week off, except for running into her at Butter.

"I got to hang out with my old friends, and we did some shopping," Paige continued. "We were walking down Avenue of the Americas, and we passed a store that was having a sample sale that we didn't even know about."

"Omigod! You totally went, right?" Alison asked.

"Of course we did!" Paige said, grinning. "We got inside, and there were, like, a zillion people fighting over clothes and purses. I grabbed a Marc Jacobs dress that was supercheap and a Chloe handbag for a ridic price."

Alison clutched her hands together. "It is seriously my dream to go to one of those. I can't wait to see your dress."

As I listened to Alison and Paige talk about the secrecy surrounding sample sales, my mind wandered to the schooling show. It's not that I didn't care about clothes—I loved shopping—but there were more important things on my mind, like doing my best on the YENT.

Mr. Davidson walked into the classroom and picked up a binder and his worn copy of *The Secret Garden* from his desk. He took his seat in our circle, running a hand over his blond hair. He was one of my favorite teachers—I'd had him last year for English and he'd pushed me into becoming a better writer and had deepened my love of books.

"Hello, everyone," Mr. Davidson said. He smiled at us, and we all smiled back. "Did you all have a good break?"

Everyone in the class nodded except for Aaron, who raised his left arm which was in a cast.

"Broke it," Aaron said. "I was at a new skate park by my house, and I lost my board on a half-pipe."

"Ouch," Mr. Davidson said. "Sorry to hear that. At least it wasn't your right arm, though. Then, we would have had to get you help with your homework." Mr. Davidson smiled.

Aaron nodded. "It would have been *so* tragic."

The entire class laughed and Mr. Davidson shot Aaron a mock stern look. But he smiled, too, and opened his notebook.

"Okay, let's get started," Mr. Davidson said. "We'll be finishing *The Secret Garden* this week, so that means you'll have a test on Monday. I'll hand out a study guide, but most of the material on the test will come from your notes."

I wrote *ENG TEST* :/ on Monday's slot in my assignment notebook.

"We'll review for the test on Friday," Mr. Davidson continued. "It'll be your last chance to ask any questions you might have about the book, and we'll run through a few potential exam questions."

"I know what *we'll* be doing all weekend," Paige whispered to me.

"Yep," I whispered back.

That *and* I'd be showing.

"Let's talk about the reading you did over break," Mr. Davidson said. "Who wants to start?"

A couple of students raised their hands, but I sat back and pretended to pay attention until the class was dismissed.

When I finally got to lunch my brain was fried. Every class had been a blur of questions, quizzes, and assignments. It was only Tuesday and teachers usually piled more work on us as the week went on. But I had to get everything done as early as I could since I wanted to devote the weekend to prepping for the show.

I stood in the lunch line, my shoulders sagging from the weight of my backpack. Today's menu was grilled cheese and fries—yum. I snagged a Diet Coke from the fridge and walked into the caf. Paige, sitting by Geena, waved me over. I glanced over toward the Trio's table and Heather caught my eye with a clear *come-sit-by-us* look.

"One sec," I mouthed to her.

I walked over to Paige, not sitting on the seat she'd pulled out for me.

"Are you going to eat standing up?" Paige teased.

Being torn between Paige and the Trio was the worst.

"No, actually, um, Heather asked if I wanted to sit with them. She invited Brit to lunch and I'm trying to make her feel welcome."

"Oh," Paige said. "I get that. I thought I noticed a look in her eye that vanished quickly. "No big deal. I'm leaving lunch early anyway and Geena and I are just going to be talking about cooking class."

"Cool," I said. "We'll catch up and talk later, okay?"

Paige smiled. "Definitely."

I turned around and started toward the Trio's table. Halfway across the cafeteria, I realized I hadn't asked Paige why she was going early. But she would have told me if it had been something important.

I slid onto the empty seat next to Alison. The Trio and Brit were already seated and starting on their lunches.

"If anyone else tells me that they didn't get a ton of homework in every class so far, I'm going to scream," Heather said.

"Agreed," Brit said. "I've got so much to do—I don't even know where to start. Classes here are intense."

"So, was your old school like this at all?" Julia asked. "You never said where you went."

I tensed waiting for Brit's answer and wondering how the Trio would react.

"Charles Middle School," Brit said, taking a bite of her grilled cheese.

The three girls paused, looking at each other.

"Charles," Julia said slowly. "Is that . . . in New York? I've never heard of it."

"Nope," Brit said, smiling. "It's in Connecticut. Sasha and I found out that we're both from small towns. We were only a few miles apart."

"Omigod," Julia said. She put her hand over her heart. "It's like you guys are long lost sisters or something." She rolled her eyes and dipped a carrot stick in blue cheese dressing.

Months ago, I would have crumpled at being treated like

that by one of the Trio. But Brit laughed. Shock replaced the smug look on Julia's face. Heather and Alison's gazes were both on Brit—neither girl seemed fazed by what Brit had just admitted.

"It *is* awesome to meet someone else from a tiny town," Brit said. "Are all you from big cities?"

Alison nodded. "New York City," she said. Her tone was nothing like Julia's had been. "But even with all the perks of living there, none of us wanted to pass up Canterwood. It definitely has the best riding program."

I just sat there, listening to them talk about the other nearby schools and how none compared to Canterwood. The only one who'd reacted at Brit's admission had been Julia. Heather wasn't making *one* comment to Brit like she'd made to me about being out of my league at Canterwood.

I forced my attention back to their conversation.

"I've been riding since I could walk," Brit said. "I clicked with Apollo the second I saw him."

"That's awesome," I said. "Because Charm and I *definitely* didn't get along too well when we first met. He threw me in the grass and galloped off. For a few minutes, I wished there was a return receipt for him."

Brit and the Trio laughed.

"Sorry to inform you, Silver, but you've got to acknowl-edge that you *still* get tossed sometimes," Heather teased.

I stuck out my tongue at Heather, not even bothering to come up with a response.

"What's your riding specialty?" Alison asked Brit.

Julia, not bothering to cover her yawn, couldn't have looked more bored.

"I love dressage," Brit said. "I've been studying it since I started riding and it's my favorite discipline."

Just like Callie, I thought. Callie, without question, was the strongest dressage rider in eighth grade.

Brit finished the final bite of her grilled cheese and checked her phone. "I've got a meeting with Ms. Utz about extracurriculars," she said. She picked up her beige tray, smiling at us. "Thanks again for inviting me to lunch."

"Invite's always open," Heather said.

Julia's face turned pink. She was treating Brit just as she'd acted toward me when Heather had first started becoming my friend. I didn't get why Julia was so worried—it's not like she was going to be forced out of the Trio.

Brit walked away from the Trio's table and left the caf. Julia leaned across the table, looking as if she was going to pounce on Heather.

"What are you doing?" Julia asked.

Heather folded her arms. "Excuse me?" Her tone was biting.

"I'm sorry, but first we let Sasha hang with us," Julia said. She acted as if I wasn't even there. "And that's fine. She *did* save Alison and me from Jasmine and I sort of trust her. But *Brit*? We don't even know her. We don't need anyone else in our group! We're the *Trio*."

Alison scraped chocolate pudding from her bowl, not looking up. My eyes flickered to Heather's face.

"Sasha isn't part of this discussion," Heather said. "And as for Brit, we want her on our side. She hasn't aligned with anyone else yet. She's a great rider. Plus, she hasn't been here long and everyone wants to be her friend."

The way Heather talked about Brit—like she was a prize or trophy—made me squirm a little.

"If everyone wants her in their group, then we need to get her on our side," Heather added. "She'll probably start her own clique if she gets the chance. And *we're* the ones who rule this grade."

"But what's so special about her?" Julia pressed.

Alison crunched on a carrot stick so loud that it was as if she was trying to break the death glare between Heather and Julia.

"If you don't like her—fine," Heather said. "There's always another seat open at a different table."

Julia's face went from red to white in half a second.

"Done eating?" Heather asked, looking at Alison and me.

I nodded and so did Alison.

We got up and, flanking Heather, left the cafeteria. And Julia.

9

THROWN

ALL THROUGH AFTERNOON CLASSES, I COULDN'T stop thinking about what had happened at lunch. Heather and Julia would make up—they'd had fights before—but I'd never seen Julia so threatened by anyone. Considering Brit had been nice to everyone since she'd gotten here, I didn't understand why Julia found her so intimidating.

I hurried back to my room after classes ended and rushed through putting on my riding clothes so I could get to the stable ASAP. Julia wasn't in my riding class, but I knew she'd be practicing. I was dying to know if she and Heather were back to being friends.

The tack room was my first stop and inside, I found Alison gathering Sunstruck's tack in her arms. *Perfect.*

"Is everything cool with Heather and Julia?" I asked. "Things got a little weird at lunch."

Alison sighed. "Yeah, that was a little intense. But they're fine now. Julia told Heather she wouldn't be mean to Brit anymore. And Julia apologized to Brit when we ran into her near the science building."

"That's good," I said. "Brit seems cool. I really like her."

"Me too," Alison said. She shifted the saddle in her arms. "Julia's always that way, though, with new people." She gave me a half smile. "You know that from experience."

"Unfortunately," I said. "You guys riding together now?"

Alison nodded. "Yep. Practicing on our own before our lesson with Mr. Conner."

"How's Cal—," I started to say, before I could stop myself.

"How's *Callie* doing in riding class?" Alison asked, her tone gentle. She understood why it was hard for me to talk about Callie.

"Yeah." My voice was quiet. "I just want to know. I mean, we're not talking, but YENT trials are coming up. I still care about her riding."

"She's doing great," Alison said. "You know Callie— she works harder than anyone and she's been so focused on riding that it shows in every practice."

I leaned against the tack room wall, both sad and happy at the same time. Focused, determined Callie was the BFF that I missed. But I was happy she was doing well in the advanced class.

Alison headed for the door. "I've got to tack up, but see you later."

"'Kay. Bye."

Alison left, closing the door behind her. Talking about Callie made me think about Jacob. On Friday, Callie would know the truth. I knew I had to let Jacob do what he wanted, but just thinking about it made me nauseous. I didn't want him to look like the bad guy because I cared about him too much. *But it's his decision,* I reminded myself.

I pulled out my phone and typed a quick message.

Want 2 meet aftr my riding lesson?

It took Jacob seconds to respond.

Of course. Txt me when ur done.

That made me smile and feel a little less sick. Just seeing him would make me feel better. More than anything, I wanted to try and see if we could make it as boyfriend and girlfriend. And, even though I hated thinking about how Callie would look at him when she knew the truth, I knew deep down that my relationship with Jacob couldn't start with lies. Not too long ago, I'd gotten caught up in lies I'd created to protect people I cared about. But they'd only ended up backfiring. Jacob was right—we had to be honest and make a clean start. I picked up Charm's tack and walked down the aisle, thinking about what I was going to do. I'd tell Paige on Friday morning too. Then, the truth about what happened at my party would spread over campus. I'd be exonerated, but Jacob . . .

Charm, always in tune with me, put his head over the stall door as I approached.

"Hi, gorgeous," I said. "Ready to work?"

Charm snorted and, laughing, I put his tack on the trunk outside his stall. I slid open his stall door and led him out in front of his stall. I glanced up and down the aisle—all of the crossties were full.

"We'll stay here, then," I told him. He didn't move as I clipped the lead line to the ring under his chin and used a slip knot to tie him to the black iron bars in front of his stall.

His coat was already shiny: Mike had groomed him after my morning lesson. All Charm needed was a quick once-over with the body brush and he was ready to be tacked up. I led him to the outdoor arena. We were warming up when Heather and Brit rode in together.

They split up, and we worked our horses in separate

spaces of the arena while we waited for Mr. Conner to arrive. Charm, high-strung, fought my hands and asked for more rein as we trotted around the arena.

I sat deeper in the saddle, trying to force my weight down into my heels.

"No," I said. "Trot."

Charm yanked his head and the reins seesawed against his neck. He tried to break into a canter, but I checked him.

What is going on with him? I thought. He was acting as if he hadn't been exercised in months.

He settled for a second, but I kept my eyes on his ears. Both of them pointed forward and I knew he wasn't listening to me. I did a half halt and pulled gently on the reins, asking him to walk. But he kept trotting and ducked his head.

"N—"

I couldn't even get the word out. Charm bucked, sending me flying through the air. I twisted in the air and landed on my shoulder like I'd been taught. But the impact of my body hitting the ground stunned me. I gasped for breath and didn't move—too shocked at what had just happened.

Hoofbeats neared me and just as I sat up, Brit and

Heather reached me with Charm in tow. Brit jumped out of her saddle while Heather held Charm.

"Are you okay?" Heather asked.

I nodded, taking a shaky breath. "Fine. Just got the wind knocked out of me."

"What happened?" Brit asked. Her wide eyes flicked over my face and her skin was pale.

"I don't know," I said, standing with help from Brit. "He wasn't listening to me when I asked him to slow. I knew he was going to buck when his head went down, but it was too late for me to stop him."

Next to Aristocrat, a contrite-looking Charm had his head low to the ground. He wouldn't look at me. He knew he'd messed up.

"It happens," Heather said. "Sometimes, there's no explanation for it. But seriously. You landed pretty hard. Do you want to see the nurse just to make sure everything's okay?"

"Aw, are you worried about me?" I asked, teasingly.

Heather rolled her eyes. "Hardly. I just don't want a lame rider on my team at the schooling show."

I moved my arms and legs, showing her that I was fine. "See? No nurse necessary. I'm ready to get back on. And *stay* on." I brushed dirt off my shoulder and pants.

I took Charm's reins from Heather and mounted. He moved at the slightest cue from me—trying to make up for what he'd done. Whatever it was, he'd gotten it out of his system because he was an angel for the rest of the warm-up.

Mr. Conner rode Lexington, a young horse he was training, into the arena. Mr. Conner on horseback meant something awesome: cross-country!

"Hi, girls," Mr. Conner said. He stopped the gray horse in front of us. "Since the weather is so nice, I thought it would be a great day for us to spend some time outside and away from the arena."

I couldn't stop my smile. That sounded *beyond* perfect.

"We're going to go for a long hack instead of taking our usual route," Mr. Conner said. Heather and I glanced at each other—we'd so do this every day if we had time.

"Follow me," Mr. Conner said. "Ready?"

"Ready," Heather, Brit, and I answered.

Instead of turning toward the woods Mr. Conner started Lexington at a walk back toward the stable yard. Brit, Heather, and I grouped together and rode behind him. Just when I thought Mr. Conner would definitely turn to the woods on the side of the stable, he kept Lexington going straight down the driveway.

"Seriously?" Heather whispered. "Are we going off campus?"

"Looks like it," I said.

Brit, riding on Heather's other side, looked over. "That would be so cool."

Riding down the driveway felt so weird. We'd never gone this way before and all three horses—especially Charm and Aristocrat—were excited. They seemed to know we were going to a new place.

The horses' shoes clinked against the driveway and I looked around, taking in the different view from Charm's back. I was so used to seeing this part of campus from the backseat of my parents' car. The pastures had gentle hills with grass cropped short by grazing horses. Every beautiful brick building that had once looked intimidating now felt like part of my home. The sun shifted from behind clouds, and I blinked as my eyes adjusted to the brighter light. The end of the driveway was near. We were rapidly approaching the road.

"Halt for a minute," Mr. Conner said.

We pulled our horses to a stop and he turned Lexington to face us. "We're going to walk the horses down the road for only a few yards before we reach a gate," he explained. "I'll open the gate, and you'll go inside the pasture. It has

ELITE AMBITION

been checked out by Mike and Doug, so it's safe. We're going to work on stamina, and we'll ride the horses at a trot and canter over a few miles of hills."

I couldn't stop a smile from spreading across my face. Riding in a new place with Charm was what we needed. I wasn't worried about him—he'd been perfect since he'd bucked me off earlier, but I'd be a little more attentive than usual just in case.

"This is a quiet road, and we've posted signs that there might be riders, so if we encounter any car traffic, the driver should be respectful," Mr. Conner said. "But stay alert and prepared just in case. Follow me single file, please."

We all nodded.

"Let's go," Mr. Conner said.

He and Lexington stepped off the driveway and onto the road. They turned right, and I went first, with Brit behind me and then Heather. The horses' shoes clanked against the asphalt—it was weird to be on the road.

Charm, calm now, kept an ear back toward me and another pointed forward. He wasn't nervous about being away from campus—he liked exploring as much as I did.

A yellow CAUTION sign with a horse and rider was posted alongside the road, but the road was deserted.

Dark wooden fences were on both sides of the street and large trees, branches sprawled over the road, cast shadows on the pavement. I turned around, grinning at Brit.

"So awesome," she mouthed at me.

I smiled, turning back around before Mr. Conner saw me.

We reached a metal gate, and he walked Lexington off the road and into the grassy shoulder. Heather, Brit, and I followed him. We watched as Mr. Conner unlatched the gate and without dismounting, opened it for us. That wasn't easy to do, especially on a semigreen horse. But Mr. Conner had been working with Lexington long enough that the gray seemed to trust him; he allowed Mr. Conner to open what probably looked like a scary gate.

Heather, Brit, and I rode through the opening, waiting while Mr. Conner relatched the gate.

"All right," Mr. Conner said, pulling Lexington next to Aristocrat. "Keep your horses at a steady canter and let's go."

I gave Charm rein and within seconds, he broke into a canter. His strides, long and even, were smooth and he kept pace with the other horses without trying to fight for the lead. He was *definitely* on his best behavior after tossing me earlier.

It felt amazing to be away from campus. There wasn't any pressure of classes, drama with Callie, or weirdness from Paige.

I shifted in the saddle, leaning forward ever so slightly as we started up a gradual incline. Charm snorted and surged forward, determined to keep the same speed going uphill as we had on the flat ground. But I didn't want Charm to strain himself, so I slowed him a notch while still allowing him to keep up with the other horses.

Brit, Heather, Mr. Conner, and I kept the horses even with each other as we climbed the easy hill. We reached the top where the ground leveled off. None of the horses were even close to being winded.

"Keep them at an easy canter," Mr. Conner said. "We have a long way to go, and I don't want anyone's horse to burn out early."

I relaxed in the saddle, enjoying the rocking gait of Charm's canter. The horses moved easily across the open field. There was nothing else I'd rather be doing. The late September air had a hint of a chill, but the sun kept me warm.

Charm's hooves made dull thuds against the grass. I'd left my hair loose under my helmet and the wind swirled it back behind me. Every stride Charm took made me feel more exhilarated. I looked over at Heather and she looked as relaxed as I felt. This was a workout for all of us, especially our horses, but it was also a release.

From everything.

Lexington tried to stick his muzzle in front of the other horses, wanting to be the one in the lead, but Mr. Conner held him back. Frustrated, Lexington shook his head, then settled.

The flat ground started to raise again, steeper this time. The horses had to work harder to keep their paces steady. I concentrated on keeping my balance and watching for any sign from Charm that he needed to slow down. But the grueling workouts with Mr. Conner had him in top shape. Brit's horse moved well, too, and we looked over at each other and smiled.

We cantered the horses up and down a few more hills before Mr. Conner slowed Lexington.

"Trot and then ease them to a walk," Mr. Conner instructed us.

Heather, Brit, and I did as he asked. Charm's copper-colored coat had darkened from sweat. His breathing was heavy, but not too hard. I was probably more ready for a break than he was!

"How do your horses feel?" Mr. Conner asked. "Is anyone sensing any strain or fatigue from her horse?"

We all shook our heads.

"Good," Mr. Conner said. "We're going to walk back to make sure they're completely cool, and we'll take a different route that's not so hilly. I don't want any of your horses to be sore before the show. That was a great workout for everyone, and I'm impressed by all of you and your horses."

Mr. Conner looked over at Brit. "I watched with how in tune you are with Apollo. You knew exactly when he needed to slow, and you never pushed him past his limits, even though you made sure the workout was a challenge. Excellent job."

"Thank you," Brit said, blushing.

I couldn't help but think if Mr. Conner had made that remark to Jasmine. Her answer would have been more of an *um, duh* than the way Brit handled the compliment— with grace. It felt surreal—like I kept expecting the cool new girl to disappear and the former princess of destruction to return.

We walked the horses back toward the stable, and I smiled to myself when I remembered who was waiting for me to finish my lesson—Jacob.

10

FRIEND, BOYFRIEND, AND MAYBE-FRIEND

BACK AT THE STABLE WITH CHARM IN CROSS-ties, I texted Jacob.

Grooming Charm. Meet in an hr under archway?

I was digging through Charm's tack box, looking for his dandy brush when my phone vibrated.

Perfect. C u there.

His text gave me chills even though I was warm from the workout.

"I'm going to meet Jacob," I whispered to Charm. "We've barely had time to talk since school started, and I really want to see him." Just saying the words made me nervous and exhilarated at the same time.

Charm, listening, turned an ear in my direction. I unclipped the crossties and led him to his stall, letting him loose inside. After I filled his water bucket, checked his hay net, and latched his stall door, he popped his head over to watch me as I gathered up his tack.

"Love you," I said.

Charm bobbed his head—his eyes connecting with mine for a second before he went for his hay net. Laughing, I stored his tack and locked myself in the stable bathroom. I ran my fingers through my hair—ridding it of the tangles from my ride. I wiped a speck of dirt off my cheek and applied a coat of peachy lip gloss. Then, I couldn't stand being in the stable for another second. Jacob was waiting for me.

I hurried down the aisle, cut across the courtyard, and headed for the stone archway. It wasn't a place of good memories, but I hoped seeing Jacob there would change that. Right now, all of my thoughts associated with the archway had to with the Belles. The then–eighth-graders had tried to force Callie, the Trio, and me into riding at midnight as part of a dare. If we completed the task, they'd coach our riding and get us invited to the coolest parties. We'd met them in a secret old room under the archway. I shivered—the memory alone was enough to make me nervous. At the final step of initiation, we'd gotten caught and, for a second, I thought I'd be sent back to Union.

Yards away from the archway, someone leaned against the stone wall. When I got closer, Jacob straightened and walked toward me, reaching for my hand. He pulled me under the arch. We were finally alone.

Together.

I'd chosen the arch because the courtyard was too public. If Jacob and I really were going to get back together, I wanted Callie to hear that and the truth from him first—not witness anything between us.

"Hi," Jacob said.

"Hi," I echoed back. My tone was high and giggly.

"I'm glad you texted me," he said. "I wanted to see you *and* make sure this is still what you want."

"It is," I said. "I can't focus too much about you telling Callie, or I'll make myself crazy. I know you're doing the right thing, but I don't want to see people looking at you the way they looked at me."

"The only person that I care about looking at me is you," Jacob said.

His words seemed to reverberate in my ears. I looked at Jacob as if I'd never seen him before—his green eyes had flecks of a half dozen shades of green that I'd never noticed before. His light brown hair looked soft and a little windswept. I wanted to reach out and touch his tan face.

"That's really sweet of you," I said. "But you have to understand where I'm coming from. I lived though the worst of it already—the whispers and stares and people gossiping about my party."

"It never should have happened," Jacob said, his jaw clenching. "I made the worst mistake by letting you take the blame. And as for the stares and whispers—like I said—I only care that you're with me. I can handle everything else."

I stared at him—wanting to kiss him but knowing better. We couldn't risk it. But once he told Callie, we were finally free to try.

"It's so weird," I said, trying to breathe evenly. "I want Friday to come and I don't. I hate the idea of stirring up talk about my party. But I'm also hopeful, whether or not it's even a possibility, that maybe Callie and I can work on our friendship again."

Jacob nodded, listening.

"I don't think we'll ever be friends again," I continued. "I mean, how can she really be friends with someone she thinks she can't trust? I *did* lie to her about what really happened, to protect her—and you. She's not just going to magically forgive me for that."

"She might not," Jacob said, touching my arm. "But

whatever happens—she needed to know the truth and you deserve to have your name cleared. It's not fair to you and it never was." He stared down at the cobblestones beneath us, then looked back at me. "I should have done something about it a long time ago. I'm sorry, Sasha. I don't know if I can apologize enough."

"Stop." I reached over and squeezed his hand for a second before letting him go. "We've been over this. You did what I asked. It's what I wanted. I should be the one apologizing to you—you need to do what feels right."

"How about we both agree to stop apologizing to each other, okay?" Jacob asked. His smile was soft.

"Okay," I said, taking a deep breath. "I can do that."

We stared at each other for minutes—neither of us saying a word. Silence was comfortable for both of us. Our bodies were inches apart, and it was almost impossible not to hug him.

Or kiss him.

More than anything—that's what I wanted to do.

"I better go," I said, reluctant. My voice broke the silence. I hated saying it, but it had to happen. No one could see us here.

A look—maybe sadness—crossed Jacob's face. But

it was replaced with understanding. "I get it," he said. "We're doing it right this time."

But the way he looked at me—I just knew. He wanted to kiss me. And, more than anything, I wanted to kiss him back.

"Right," I said. I took a tiny step back. The longer I was closer to him—the harder it was to step away.

"Text you later," Jacob said, squeezing my arm then letting me go. I half wished he'd kept his hand on my arm and forced me to stay. But we both knew better.

"Okay. Bye." I tore my eyes away from his and left the archway, leaving him standing there.

Hours later, I sat down to dinner in the caf. My brain was still stuck on what had gone on earlier with Jacob. The scene kept replaying in front of my eyes—the light breeze that had blown the scent of fresh cut grass through the archway, the warmth that seemed to radiate from Jacob's body and—what I couldn't forget no matter how hard I tried—the way he'd looked when I'd approached him. I couldn't help but worry about the timing of everything. Jacob was telling Callie the truth before the schooling show, which was important to her. I blinked and flashed back to when I'd been testing for the YENT and had found out that Callie and Jacob were together. It had almost ruined my chances at making the team. I didn't want this show to be a mess for Callie. Not after I knew how it felt.

I stirred my wonton soup, usually one of my faves when the caf served Chinese food. But today I was unable to focus enough to eat without spilling soup down my shirt.

"Everything okay?" Paige asked. She finished her third pork dumpling and wiped her mouth.

"Totally fine," I said. I directed my gaze from my soup to Paige's face. "I had a big lunch."

Paige nodded. "Gotcha. I did, too, but I love Chinese food so much and . . ."

She kept talking but her words stopped registering in my brain when I saw two people walk through the doorway.

Eric. Rachel.

Something overwhelming came over me—I couldn't sit another second without talking to Eric. I had no idea what to even say, but I couldn't stop myself.

"I'll be right back," I said to Paige.

"Okaaay," she said. "Are you all right?"

"Great," I said. "I'll just . . . be right back."

And without explanation, I got up and headed for Eric

and Rachel. They approached the lunch line, whispering to each other as they got closer. Eric, with his light brown skin and dark hair, looked more ready for a casting call than class. Rachel had a classic girl-next-door look—pretty and petite with light brown hair and natural reddish highlights.

"Hi," I said to both of them.

"Hey," Eric and Rachel said, both smiling at me. I didn't pick up on a hit of weirdness or jealousy from Rachel that I was talking to my ex.

"I'm going to grab my tray," Rachel said, laughing. "There's no way I'm missing any of the sweet-and-sour chicken." Maybe she knew I wanted a minute alone with Eric. Rachel and I weren't even close to friends, but she was being gracious. I don't know if I could handle myself as well as she was in this situation.

Eric smiled at Rachel. "Be right there."

We looked at each other, my nerves started to calm the longer I looked at him.

"How're you doing?" Eric asked. His dark brown eyes, gentle like always, were sincere as he looked at me.

"Good," I said. "Fall break was fun. How about you?"

"Busy," he said, brushing back his dark brown hair. "I'm riding Luna as much as I can. Sometimes it feels like I'm living in the stable."

I laughed. "Tell me about it. I think Charm was secretly glad to see me go over break."

"No, never." Eric joined my laughter.

I shifted, swallowing. "I didn't mean to interrupt your lunch. I just wanted to say that you've always been such a great friend to me. I miss seeing you."

"I miss talking to you too," Eric said.

"You're a good guy, and I don't want things to be weird between us. I'm—" The next part was harder to get out. "I'm glad you've got Rachel. She seems cool and I want you to be happy. I just hope . . . that, somehow, we can still be friends."

The last part of the sentence gushed out. But I meant it. I needed Eric in my life. No more drama. Or wars between Jacob and Eric. Just all of us coexisting at school and getting back to our normal lives.

"I want that, too, Sasha," Eric said. He glanced at the cafeteria floor, then back at me. "We both went through rough things. Maybe the timing wasn't right for us—I don't know. But I care about you as a friend. I want to talk. The avoiding-each-other thing is ridiculous."

Relief dizzied me—almost forcing me to grab the table beside me.

"I'm so glad you feel that way. Really. And I want to know how riding's going. Maybe we can, I don't know, practice together sometime or something?"

Eric nodded. "I'd love that. Luna misses Charm—you know she had a crush on him."

We both laughed. "It was mutual," I said. "Well, go grab lunch, and I'll see you around."

Eric and I traded smiles. As I walked back to rejoin Paige, I felt better about the possibilities of the future than I had in weeks. Eric and I were on track to becoming friends. Paige and I *would* get back our super-BFF status. Jacob and I were going to start dating. And, either the best or the worst of all of these things, Callie would know the truth—in less than four days.

II

QUEEN
OF DRESSAGE

couldn't come fast enough. It was only the third day back to class, but it felt like break hadn't even happened and I'd been studying fractions and American history *forever*. All I wanted to do was ride.

I pushed open the tack room door and found Brit inside, wiping off the cantle of her saddle.

"Hey," I said. "Ready for another 'easy' lesson at Canterwood?"

Brit grinned, putting her saddle cloth in a nearby bucket. "You know it. I mean, c'mon. Mr. Conner needs to step up the difficulty a little."

"He totally does," I said, laughing. We picked up our tack and, together, walked out of the tack room.

"How're your classes?" I asked. "Those supereasy too?"

Brit groaned. "Seriously. I might drown in homework. Were you overwhelmed when you came here?"

"That's an understatement," I said. "I was *beyond* overwhelmed. I had no friends, the classes were super-intimidating, and I was trying to make the advanced riding team."

Brit shifted the bridle on her shoulder. "How did you get through it? I'm kind of scared that I won't make it with grades *and* riding."

"You can," I said, looking at her. "There were a million times when I got here that I wanted to quit and go home. But I finally learned how to juggle everything—it just took time. Same for you, I'm sure. Just give it a little while and you'll see."

That seemed to put Brit at ease. She smiled, the worry gone from her eyes. "Thanks, Sasha. That really makes me feel better, especially coming from someone who's gone through it."

"No problem. And if you need help with classes, let me know. If I can't help, I'm sure I know someone who can."

"I definitely will."

We smiled at each other, and Brit reached Apollo's

stall. "Hey, want to grab dinner tonight? I heard about this pizza place on campus that sounds *so* good."

"The Slice is awesome," I said. "Meet you there around seven?"

"Perfect."

I left Brit with Apollo and headed to see Charm. I put down his tack on his trunk, and he stuck his head over the door, watching me.

"What's up, guy?" I asked him. "Ready for our lesson?"

Charm blinked, seeming to contemplate my question.

"Oh," I said, my tone teasing. "You thought I was coming to turn you out, huh?"

"Turn out" were words Charm understood. He bobbed his head, flapping his lower lip. I laughed. "Sorry. No grazing right now. You can do that tomorrow while I'm in class."

I opened the stall door, leading him into the aisle. I clipped him into a pair of crossties and took his tack box from the trunk.

It only took a few minutes to groom him—he hadn't rolled outside or gotten dusty since this morning's grooming. After tacking him up and putting on my helmet, I led him to the indoor arena.

We were the first ones inside, soon followed by

Heather and then Brit. Each of us focused on warming up our horse—no one said a word. Heather had switched Aristocrat's usually white saddle pad for a hunter green one that made the chestnut's coat look even darker.

We walked and trotted the horses for almost fifteen minutes before Mr. Conner walked inside.

"Hello, everyone," he said with a nod. "It's good to see you all here."

We echoed back hellos and waited for instruction from him.

"Today," Mr. Conner said. "We're going to work on dressage."

I didn't need to look at Brit to know she was smiling. Dressage was her favorite discipline, and she hadn't had a chance to show off her skills yet. I couldn't wait to see her and Apollo in action.

"Sitting trot, everyone," Mr. Conner said.

Brit, Heather, and I all sat to our horses' trots, and I noticed how smooth Brit was in the saddle. She barely moved at all.

"Change directions," Mr. Conner called.

We crossed over the center of the arena. Brit sat for a beat to stay on the right diagonal, and Apollo went right to the opposite rail like he was supposed to. I couldn't stop watching Brit—her hands were still, her legs stayed in the correct position and her shoulders were back, but her back wasn't ramrod straight.

And, by the end of the lesson, I still hadn't seen any mistakes. Brit and Apollo had been stars in every area Mr. Conner put us though—from a working trot to half-passes. I hadn't seen anyone do dressage moves like that since I'd watched Callie ride. Brit's skills in the saddle were something I think even Heather had to marvel at.

"That was a great lesson," Mr. Conner said. "I expect all of you to work on the areas we discussed. You're all progressing in the direction I'd hoped for the schooling show. I have no doubt that Mr. Nicholson will be impressed with all of your hard work."

The last sentence eased some of the anxiety in my chest. Mr. Conner didn't just say things he didn't mean. If he thought we weren't going to be ready or if he had concerns about the show, he'd be telling us. But what he said made me hopeful that if Charm and I kept working at the pace we did, we'd be prepared for Sunday's show.

"Cool down your horses, and I'll see you tomorrow," Mr. Conner said.

Heather, Brit, and I dismounted. We walked our horses in large, lazy circles in the arena until they were cool and dry. Heather waved at both of us as she took Aristocrat out of the arena. I walked Charm for a few more minutes before deciding it was time to groom him.

"See you tonight," I said to Brit.

"Bye," she said.

12

LIAR, LIAR

"THAT'S COOL THAT YOU'RE MEETING BRIT for pizza," Paige said, half yelling. I was drying my hair, and she was flatironing hers.

"It'll be fun," I said. I turned off the hair dryer and starting pulling my hair into sections to flatiron it. "It's like I've known her forever, and we keep finding out that we have more in common than we thought every time we hang out."

I sprayed my hair with Bumble and Bumble Prep spray and grabbed my already hot flatiron. "And you're *definitely* going to have fun tonight," I said. "Are you superexcited about meeting Ryan?"

Paige nodded. "Yeah. Really excited."

I unclipped another section of my hair, waiting for her to gush.

"Sooo . . ." I asked, "where are you guys going? What are you wearing?"

Paige seemed concentrated on her hair. "Oh. We can't decide. We might see a movie, but neither of us could make up our minds."

"Oooh, so it's like a spontaneous date," I said. "Fun!"

Paige ran her fingers through her red hair and sprayed it with finishing gloss. "Totally. And are you coming right back after The Slice?"

I nodded. "Pretty sure. I'm kind of tired after the lesson today. Plus, I've got a math quiz tomorrow, and I don't want to fall asleep during class."

"Cool," Paige said. "We'll meet back here then, okay?"

"Definitely."

We finished our hair, checked each other's makeup, and left Winchester. Paige headed for Blackwell, Ryan's dorm, and I walked toward The Slice.

The lanterns had flickered on and illuminated campus. Going out for pizza felt like the right middle-of-the-week way to relax—I couldn't wait to get there and chill. I reached The Slice, catching my reflection in the doorway. I'd paired skinny jeans with ankle boots and a long-sleeve plum shirt.

I pulled open the door, the smell of pizza and garlic

bread wafting around me. I loved the old-fashioned shop. All of the tables were covered with red and white checkered tablecloths with mini-lanterns in the center of the tables. The lighting was soft and the entire vibe felt chill. My favorite part was the pizza-making counter, shielded by glass, where the staff tossed dough high in the air, caught it, then covered the pizza in sauce, cheese, and the patron's topping of choice.

Someone waved at me, and I saw Brit had already grabbed a table. Seated with her were Heather, Julia, and Alison.

"Sorry to crash your date," Heather said, grinning. "But we were in the mood for pizza too."

"Cool," I said.

But the look on Julia's face definitely did *not* look cool. Instead, she looked as if she wished The Slice had never existed. But after her smackdown with Heather, I doubted that she'd complain. Silent pouting was way more mature.

A waiter came, and we all ordered sodas and cheesy breadsticks before we ordered pizza.

"Is this not, like, the longest week ever?" Alison moaned. She leaned back in the red booth.

"It so is," Brit said. "Sasha and I were talking about

that at the stable. It's so overwhelming and intimidating to think about all of the work we have to get done."

Heather sighed. "You guys need to relax. Seriously. Especially you, Silver. You've survived this long—not that I know how you did—I think you're going to make it." She looked at Brit. "And you'll get used to things. It's only your first week here. It'll get easier."

"Hopefully," Brit said, her smile tentative.

The waiter, who had to be one of Canterwood's high school students, came with our drinks and set a plate of steaming breadsticks in the middle of the table.

We all dove for them—our hands bumping together. Everyone laughed.

"Omigod, it's like we've never eaten in public before," Heather said, holding back a smile. It kept getting easier to spot her fake-annoyance.

We took turns taking breadsticks for the basket, and it didn't take long for the Canterwood gossip to start. Julia, and especially Alison, knew *everything* that was going on in school.

"Did you hear that Danielle on our floor broke up with Justin for the *third* time?" Alison asked.

"No!" We all chorused. Danielle and I'd been in a class together last year, but we hadn't talked much.

"I mean, c'mon! It's 'I like you, then I don't' and just this back-and-forth. It's, like, omigod, stop already!" Alison rubbed her temples, her lilac nail polish gleaming in the light. "Either be together or stay broken up. It's ridic."

I'd be a total hypocrite if I commented on that. My situation with Eric wasn't like Danielle's where I kept breaking up with the same boyfriend over and over, but I had almost been Jacob's girlfriend, and then not, so many times.

"There must be something there," Brit said. She played with the long dangling silver necklace she'd looped twice around her neck.

We paused the conversation when the waiter came over and set the pizza in the middle of us. The half cheese, half pepperoni pizza looked delish. I was so hungry, I probably could have devoured the entire thing. I grabbed a giant slice of pepperoni.

Once everyone had a slice, Heather looked at Brit. "What were you going to say?"

Brit shook pepper flakes onto her pizza and took a sip of soda.

"I was saying that, yeah, they keep breaking up and getting back together, but nobody would keep doing that to themselves if there weren't feelings involved. Danielle and Justin must feel *something* for each other that keeps drawing them to each other."

"That's kind of romantic," Julia said, taking a giant bite of pizza. "They can't stay away from each other even when they try."

Looking at me for the briefest of seconds, Heather glanced back at the group. "It sounds like she needs to make up her mind. Danielle has to know she wants to be with him, and they need to stop wasting time and be together."

I coughed on my sip of soda, covering my mouth with my hand before I spewed it all over the table. Some of it dropped from my hand onto the table.

"Silver! Gross!" Heather said. She shook her head, handing me a stack of napkins.

Clearly she'd been talking about *me*. That I needed to make a commitment to try a relationship with Jacob if that's what I wanted. Heather had known I'd gone back and forth about my feelings for Jacob and Eric—worried about hurting both guys that I cared about in different ways. But, deep down, I knew Jacob and I had missed our chance at something that had potential to be amazing.

And I wanted that opportunity now.

"I can't even imagine breaking up with Ben," Julia continued. The soft lighting in our spot in the pizza parlor made her blond hair shine softly.

Alison elbowed her, teasingly. "I can't wait to have someone to worry about breaking up with or not."

Everyone, including Alison, laughed.

"You'll find the right guy," Heather said. "It's good to be choosy. I mean, it's not as if you could be part of the Trio if you were dating a loser."

Alison's eyes widened and hand froze with her slice of pizza halfway to her mouth.

"Kidding, you dork," Heather said, patting her friend's shoulder. "As if we'd ever *let* a loser dude anywhere near you."

That made Alison smile. And it was true—the Trio protected each other.

"What about you guys?" Brit asked, looking at Heather and me. "Are you seeing anyone? Got any crushes?"

I shoved pizza into my mouth, forcing Heather to speak first. She gave me a pointed look, knowing exactly what I was doing. I kept chewing verrry slowly.

"There's a guy," Heather said slowly. "We really just started talking over break, and it's too early to tell anything since we haven't been out yet, but we'll see."

I sat back a little, surprised that she'd revealed anything to Brit.

Brit looked over at me. "What about you?"

Heather stared back at me like, and-now-it's-your-turn-go.

"Um, well, I'm not . . . dating anyone right now," I said. That was the truth, mostly. I didn't want to tell Brit about the Jacob situation before he talked to Callie. Brit seemed trustworthy, but I couldn't risk it. Every move between Jacob and me until he talked to Callie had to be supercareful. And he wouldn't be talking to her until Friday.

"Welcome to the club, then," Brit said, smiling. "I just got to Canterwood, so I'm obviously without a guy. There are tons of cute boys here, but I need at least, oh, another week to settle in before I start looking."

She tossed her hair in a flirty motion and grinned.

"I wish we all lived in Orchard!" Brit said, sticking out her bottom lip. "We'd have so much fun. I have a double—we could *so* be roomies!"

"It would be great," I admitted. "My roommate and I are having some problems right now, but she's still my best friend. I know we're going to work it out."

"Well, we can at least do sleepovers sometimes," Brit said.

"For sure."

But as I ate my pizza, I wasn't so sure about Paige and me. Things with Paige had shifted since the night of our blowup. I couldn't shake the feeling that she wasn't telling me something. Maybe she was still mad that I'd chosen to stay at Heather's for spring break. If that was true I wish she'd tell me instead of being weird. It just made me paranoid, and it couldn't be healthy for her to hold it in.

"Sleepovers would definitely be awesome," I said. "I'm in."

We finished our pizza and Heather, Julia, and Alison put cash on the table.

"We're going to the media center to watch a movie," Heather said. "See you guys later."

Brit and I said bye to them and took final sips of our sodas.

"Want to grab dessert at The Sweet Shoppe?" I asked. "I heard that hazelnut chocolate cake is on the menu."

"Hmmm . . ." Brit put a finger to her chin, the smile on her face giving away her answer. "Such a tough decision. I'm never able to pass up chocolate cake."

"Me either," I said. "It's an illness, or something."

We paid the bill and left The Slice.

"I like Alison, Julia, and Heather," Brit said. "What's your deal with them?"

"A pretty messy history," I said, blowing out a huge breath. "Heather hated me the second I got to campus. Charm spooked and ran away from me on my first day. He scared Aristocrat and Heather fell off."

Brit blinked a bunch of times. "Omigod. Was she hurt?"

"No, just really, *really* angry," I said. "She wouldn't let it go for a long time, and she took every chance she got to get back at me. We hated each other, and, because of Heather's behavior toward me, Julia and Alison weren't exactly nice either."

"Yeaaah," Brit said. "Julia acts like she wishes I would disappear. But Heather and Alison have been cool to me, so I hope it rubs off on Julia."

"Total mystery with that girl," I said, shaking my head. "I've seen her go back and forth all the time. You can never be sure. All you can do is keep hanging with Alison and Heather, since you seem to like them, and hopefully Julia will get over whatever her problem is."

"Fingers crossed," Brit said. "We'll have to have a sleepover in my room some time and maybe if I get Julia's favorite movie or food, she'll be a little nicer."

I grinned. "Oh, Brit. It'll take a lot more than that to get Julia on your side."

We walked under the blue and white awning of The Sweet Shoppe and opened the door. Scents of brownies, cookies, cakes and other delicious treats filled the shop. I inhaled as deeply as possible, taking in the smell of yummy desserts. If I wasn't afraid of going into a sugar coma I'd live at The Sweet Shoppe. Everything was tempting from the zillions of ice cream flavors (bubblegum and Superman—hello!) to the varieties of hot chocolate with real whipped cream on top.

"Have you been here before?" I asked Brit.

"I've walked past it a zillion times, but I've never stopped inside," she said. She looked around at shop. It was adorable with booths, tables, and comfy chairs. The Shoppe was full of windows, and I loved looking at all of the gallons of ice cream that were under the glass counter.

"I'm sooo in the mood for an ice cream sundae right now," I said. "Hot fudge, cherries . . . yum."

"Oooh, that does sound awesome," Brit said. "And with nuts on top—perfect."

We stepped up to the counter. There were a couple of people in front of us, so we waited in line. The Sweet Shoppe was never *not* busy. Everyone came here and . . .

I jerked my head toward a window booth near the back where I heard a familiar laugh. Paige, spooning yogurt parfait into her mouth, was sitting with her back to me. Sitting across from her? *Definitely* not Ryan.

Callie.

Callie. My ex-BFF Callie who swore she'd never speak to me again. Paige and Callie had been friends for a while, and I didn't care if they hung out. I *did* care that Paige had made me think she was going to see Ryan. How many times had she been meeting "Ryan" when it had really been Callie?

"You okay?" Brit asked, nudging my arm.

I yanked my gaze away from the table, glad that Callie hadn't noticed me yet.

"Totally," I said. "Just saw my roommate."

Brit frowned. "The one you're having trouble with, right?"

I sighed, wishing the line would disappear so Brit and I could grab our desserts and split.

"Yeah. She's here with my ex–best friend. Which is fine. It's always been cool with me that they're friends."

Brit paused for a second. "But?"

"But she lied about meeting her boyfriend, and instead, she's here with Callie. If they're going to hang out, it's truly okay with me. Paige knows me better than that. She knows I don't mind if she and Callie are friends, but she doesn't have to lie."

My last word almost made me gag. Hypocrite much? I'd lied so much, thinking I was protecting my friends, and it had all blown up in my face. That's why I couldn't be mad at Paige for lying. But I felt something, maybe jealousy, that Paige and Callie were friends. Even after all we'd been through, I still hoped Callie and I could be friends again.

We got up to the counter, and I didn't look in their direction again. While Brit ordered, I could pick Callie and Paige's laughter amidst the murmur of voices.

"Do you want me to grab our food, and you can wait outside?" Brit asked. "I don't mind."

"Thanks, but I'm okay," I said. I tried to pay attention to Brit, but my mind was on Callie. After Jacob told her the truth about what had really happened at my party, I wondered if she'd want to talk. But part of me knew better—I was going to be dating her ex. Her first boyfriend. There was no way she'd talk to me.

"Sasha?" Brit asked.

"Oh, sorry." I looked up at the barista. "I'll take an ice cream sundae to go, please."

Brit ordered the same, and we stepped to the side to wait. I kept my gaze away from Callie and Paige. It was so busy in here, I didn't know if Callie had spotted me or not. If she had, she wasn't showing it.

"Are you going to talk to Paige about seeing her here?" Brit asked, keeping her voice low.

I shrugged. "I really don't know. I kind of want her to come to me first. Our friendship is a little weird right now. I don't want to make a big deal out of her hanging with Callie, but I want her to know she doesn't have to hide it from me."

The barista brought us our sundaes, we paid and took the bags, heading outside.

"Want to sit at the picnic tables?" Brit asked.

"Perf," I said.

Brit didn't bring up the Callie-and-Paige drama again as we walked to the wooden picnic tables just down the hill from The Sweet Shoppe. The sun was starting to set, and the campus's streetlamps flickered on.

No one else was sitting at any of the tables, so we picked one and sat.

I peeled off the lid of my sundae container and dug my plastic spoon into a bite of chocolate ice cream and a bit of banana.

The darkness closing in around us made me feel safe and as if the drama had disappeared. At least for a little while. This part of the grounds made me feel that way.

"This campus is so gorgeous," Brit said.

I smiled, glad for the distraction.

"I know," I said. "I was so overwhelmed by it when I first got here. I'd never been to a school like this—I wanted to see every inch of it all at once."

"I get that," Brit said. "I've walked everywhere and gotten lost sooo many times."

"Ooh, there's one thing you haven't done. It's, like, a requirement if you ride."

Brit put down her spoon. "Spill."

"Trail ride!" I said. "I mean, c'mon. You have to see the trails and everything. Plus, it's so much fun to trail ride around here."

"I *love* trail riding," Brit said. She took a giant bite of strawberry ice cream. "I've been dying to go since I got here, but I didn't want to get lost."

"Want to go after our lesson tomorrow?" I asked. "Promise not to get you lost."

"Deal."

Brit and I tapped our spoons together, giggling, and dug back into our ice cream.

13

TWO. MORE. DAYS.

THE NEXT MORNING PAIGE AND I GOT READY
for class as if nothing had happened the night before.
When I'd gotten back to my room last night, I'd been
in such a good mood from hanging with Brit that
I'd decided to let Paige come to me about Callie.
I didn't want to create any more rifts between us. Paige
would tell me—I knew she would. I'd kept the entire
Jacob-tried-to-kiss-me-at-my-party truth from her for
so long that I wasn't in a place to confront her about
lying.

"I'm *so* tired," Paige said. She stuck an armful of textbooks into her messenger bag. "At least it's Thursday.
Two. More. Days."

Or, one more day until Jacob told Callie the truth.

"I know. You'd think we'd be used to the workload by now, but nope," I said.

I sneaked a glance at Paige. This morning's small talk was weird. Usually, we talked about boys or accessories or fun things. But so far, all Paige had wanted to talk about was how tired she was and how classes were keeping her crazy busy. Something felt . . . off.

Paige finished packing her books as I put on a pair of silver hoops.

"You doing anything after class?" I asked. "I'm trail riding with Brit after our lesson, then chaining myself to my desk to do homework."

"Same on the homework part," Paige said. "I might meet Geena or something, but I don't know yet. She might be too busy."

I wanted to ask her about Callie, but I kept my mouth shut. Paige would talk to me. I just had to wait.

Later that afternoon I slid into an empty seat during math class. Brit wasn't here yet. My phone buzzed, and I opened it to see a text from Jacob.

Knw ur in class but wanted 2 say hi.

Just seeing his name made me think about tomorrow. Today felt like it would never end. Every minute felt stretched, and I both wanted tomorrow to come and never get here at the same time. Each time I thought about Jacob telling Callie, I felt hot and cold at the same time with no idea of the outcome.

I started to type back, but closed my phone when Brit walked over.

"Hey," she said.

"Hi."

I needed someone to distract me from my worries about Jacob and Callie. And if anyone could do it—it would be Brit.

Brit looked chic but appropriate for class in black leggings, gold ballet flats, and a long-sleeve royal blue sweater. She placed her textbook and homework on her desk, then leaned closer to me.

"How's your day been so far?" Brit asked.

"Busy," I said. "I swear I've been assigned more home-work in every class than I ever have since I started. It's like all I do is complain about homework, but it's so true!"

Brit nodded. "Same here. I'm feeling a little pressure with school, training, and trying to have *some* time to relax."

"Maybe we should think about a study group or some-thing," I said. "I know I stay focused better when other people around me are working too."

"That's a great idea," Brit said. "We can talk about it over the weekend, maybe, and then tell people about it."

Ms. Utz walked in, almost having to duck under the doorway because she was so tall. Brit and I smiled at each other, and I felt a little less anxious. At least I'd get my homework back under control soon.

After math I walked down the hallway, jamming books into my bag. I rounded the corner and almost ran right into Eric.

"Sorry!" I said.

He reached out to steady me, then quickly pulled away his hand.

"No big deal," he said. He looked cute today in a red polo shirt and jeans.

"How are things?" I asked. That seemed like an easy question to start easing back into a friendship with.

"Good," he said, shifting his backpack. "Busy, but like that ever changes. How about you?"

"Same," I said. "Riding a lot."

"Me too. Luna's doing really great." When Eric said her name, I saw a familiar sparkle in his eye.

"That's awesome!" And I meant it. I was still invested in Eric as a rider. "We'll have to practice together some- time and catch up on each other's skills."

Eric laughed. "Definitely. I've got class, but see you later."

He walked past me, leaving me smiling for the first time in a while.

"I've never been so happy to see anyone in my life," I said to Charm, putting his tack on the trunk outside his stall. I'd made it through the rest of my classes, but hadn't been able to concentrate. As much as I tried, I couldn't stop thinking about tomorrow.

I let myself into Charm's stall and hugged his neck. "Ugh," I moaned. "I'm so nervous! Jacob's telling Callie the truth tomorrow. Her experience with her first *ever* boyfriend is now going to be even more ruined. And I care about Jacob so much, and I don't like to think about Callie being mad at him."

Charm gazed at me, almost as if he was encouraging me to keep talking. "And I don't know if Callie will forgive me for lying to her about that," I said. "I know friends fight sometimes, but Callie and I have gone through a *lot* of fights since I got to school. But we never gave up on each other because our friendship was too important. We let a boy get between us—something I never wanted to happen."

I went quiet for a minute, everything running through my head. Forcing myself, I took a shaky breath and led Charm out of his stall.

I retrieved Charm's tack box from his trunk and went to work on his coat. Crouching down I brushed away bits of hay that clung to his legs, then grabbed his hoof pick with a red, rubber-coated handle. Charm stood still as I scraped away bits of dirt from his hooves and around his horseshoe.

"Hey, Sasha," Mike said. "Mr. Conner had a last-minute meeting pop up and there won't be any afternoon lessons. Riders who want to practice can ride in any of the arenas as long as there's no jumping without a partner."

"Okay," I said. "Thanks."

I definitely wanted to jump and had no doubt Heather did too. Scanning the aisle, I spotted her a few stalls away.

"Outdoor arena?" I called. My voice was barely audible over the sound of the usual stable noises of horses nickering, hooves clicking down the aisle, and other students chatting.

"Def!" Heather called back.

I went back to picking Charm's hooves, then stopped. There were no lessons today. That meant anyone who wanted to ride could end up in the same arena.

ELITE AMBITION

Eric.

Rachel.

Callie.

Julia and Alison.

Stop it, I told myself, shaking my head. I was being ridiculous. There were a half dozen arenas and the odds of me ending up in one with Callie or Eric was slim. *Plus,* I reminded myself, *you and Eric made a pact to be friends.* And I really did want our friendship to continue.

I hadn't seen him ride in a while. And I wanted to see how he was doing with Luna—especially after we'd practiced together so much before our breakup. Even thinking about the flea-bitten gray mare made me miss riding with Eric. Charm and Luna had always gotten along, and Luna, a school horse, was the perfect match for Eric.

If Callie was in the arena . . . she'd ignore me anyway. But thinking about riding with Callie still made my stomach gurgle. It was hard to ride with someone I knew hated me. At least I had Heather in the arena.

I finished tacking up Charm, snapped on my helmet and led him down the aisle. I stopped Charm by Aristocrat as Heather put on her black helmet and, together, we walked the horses down the aisle.

"When Mike told me that our lesson was canceled,"

Heather said. "I thought I'd be upset. But I'm actually kind of glad to work on whatever I want. It'll be good before the schooling show."

"Agreed," I said. "I know what Charm and I need to do. I'm glad you wanted to work outside because I needed a jumping partner."

"As if you're the only one who wants to jump."

We halted the horses just outside the stable and mounted. Charm and Aristocrat walked over the grass, both horses relaxed with their ears flicking back and forth and their strides even. Months ago, Charm would have sidestepped to get away from Aristocrat, or Heather's horse would have put back his ears back and shot Charm a mean look.

The closer Heather and I became, the less tension there was between our horses. It was definitely better for us as a team if *everyone*—horses included—got along.

We approached the large outdoor arena where a black horse cantered in large circles.

Black Jack.

The horse did a flying lead change as if he could do it all day and crossed over the center of the arena. Suddenly, I didn't know if I could ride with Callie. Even from the entrance the arena felt tiny. Claustrophobia about riding with Callie was taking over.

"Heather," I whispered. "Maybe we should ride in another arena. It looks like Callie's having a serious practice."

Heather shook her head, keeping Aristocrat moving toward the arena. "Callie's not intimidating you out of the arena. You're not going to have a talk show moment where you break down, hug, and forgive each other. You're going to *ride*."

Heather's comment made me smile.

"You're right," I said. "We're all here to practice. There's no reason to talk or anything."

"Exactly. Now get focused and let's go."

Heather let Aristocrat into a faster walk, which made Charm want to catch up. Heather and I approached the dark wooden rail fencing. I didn't want to stare at Callie, but I couldn't help it. We hadn't had a lesson together since I'd made the YENT and she hadn't.

Every riding skill of Callie's that I'd thought had been near perfect was now razor sharp. Callie was going to make the YENT this time. I knew it. Julia and Alison, though both excellent riders, had a tiny chance if that. Callie must have channeled every feeling she'd had about the breakup with Jacob into riding. Her focus had paid off in every way.

"Nice," Heather said under her breath. "Julia and Alison better be out here practicing."

All I could manage was a nod. Callie slowed Black Jack to a trot and the Morab tossed his mane, snorting. Charm's ears pointed toward Black Jack—he wanted to practice alongside his friend. But I held him back near Aristocrat.

Callie looked up, spotting Heather and me. There wasn't a bit of animosity or annoyance on her face— instead, she just looked at us with a cool gaze. She turned Black Jack in a circle, then let him into a collected trot.

"Hey, guys."

Heather and I looked over to see Brit slow her horse beside Charm.

"Hey," Heather and I said.

"Is there enough room for me to ride in here too?" Brit asked. She held the reins with one hand and adjusted her helmet with the other. "I'm not going to jump—I just want to work on dressage."

"There's plenty of room," Heather said. "Go for it."

Brit flashed a smile and walked Apollo in front of us to an empty corner of the arena.

"Let's go," Heather said to me. "I'm not spending this entire time staring at Callie. We're here to ride."

"Right," I said. After one more deep breath, I squeezed my legs against Charm's sides and he walked forward. Heather and I walked, trotted, and cantered the horses, taking our time to make sure they were warmed up. A couple of times I caught Heather watching Troy, her crush, exercise his horse a few arenas away.

"Coach my jumping first?" Heather asked. "Then, I'll critique you."

"Deal," I said, glancing over to see how Brit and Callie were doing. The girls were directly across from each other at the same end of the arena. Callie was doing stretches in her saddle, her feet kicked out of the stirrups.

Her eyes were focused on Brit.

I shifted my gaze to Brit and saw why. Brit and Apollo were working on leg yielding. I couldn't even see Brit cuing Apollo to move. He seemed to shift from invisible signals from her—as if he read her mind and knew what she wanted. Callie had been the best dressage rider in our grade. No question and everyone knew it. But Brit was *good*. As good as Callie. Maybe better. Now, Callie had competition for the YENT with Julia and Alison and a drive to be the best at dressage against Brit.

"Silver!"

Heather's sharp tone made me yank my gaze away from

Callie and Brit. Heather was waiting a few yards from the start of the jump course.

"Sorry," I said. "Coming!"

Don't get involved, I told myself. If any tension between Brit and Callie surfaced over dressage, it wasn't my fight. It would probably push Callie that much harder to practice more—if that was even possible. Plus, I didn't expect Brit to be anything less than professional.

I stopped Charm near the middle of the six-jump course. Mr. Conner and Mike changed the jumps almost every week, and Charm and I hadn't practiced on this one yet.

"Can you focus for five minutes, or do I need to find someone else to watch me ride?" Heather asked. She tilted her head as she looked at me.

"I'm focused!" I said. "Seriously. Start whenever you want. I'm ready."

Heather stared at me for what felt like forever before she pushed her heel against Aristocrat's side and turned him away from the course. She asked him to trot, then let him into an easy canter. I kept my gaze on Heather's posture and the way Aristocrat moved. They were such a tight pair that I knew their mistakes, if any, would be minor. The course wasn't especially challenging either. But it would provide a good workout for us.

Charm seemed to sense that we'd be going soon and that he was watching his competition. Even though the horses were still on the same team—they were competitive with each other.

Heather guided Aristocrat toward the first jump. The gelding tucked his knees gracefully under his body and jumped without hesitation. He looked gorgeous suspended, for even a millisecond, over the red and white rails. Mr. Conner and Mike hadn't left much room between the first jump and another vertical that was taller than the first. But Heather and Aristocrat were ready. Heather lifted slightly out of the saddle at just the right moment, sliding her hands along Aristocrat's neck. Aristocrat took the higher jump as if it was the same height as the first.

Heather guided him over an oxer, another vertical, and a second oxer. I kept my focus on both of them, looking for any missteps. But Aristocrat and Heather *owned* the course. They cantered in a half circle, preparing for the last vertical. The hunter green and gold poles were higher than any of the previous jumps on the course. Aristocrat, excited by the jump, moved at a faster clip—rushing the jump. Heather's fingers closed around the reins and she did a half halt, asking him to slow.

Aristocrat slowed, listening to Heather's cue, but

still took off a few inches too close to the jump. His knees knocked the top rail and it tumbled to the ground. Heather let him canter for a few more strides before pulling him to a trot, then finally a walk. She patted his neck, but shook her head.

"What's the verdict?" Heather asked.

I shifted in the saddle. "It was a perfect round until the final jump. Aristocrat didn't respond in time to your cue, so maybe you need to work him through a refresher with flatwork and then try the course again."

Heather nodded. "That's a good idea. What about my posture?"

"Your legs slid too far forward a few times, but, otherwise, you were great."

Heather smiled. "Thanks. After I watch you jump, I'll do flatwork."

"Sounds good."

I asked Charm to walk and moved him away from the course. Like Aristocrat, Charm had a tendency to get excited on courses. We moved through a few circles before I held him at an easy, slow canter up to the first vertical. Just like Aristocrat, Charm flew over the first jump and the next vertical. His attention was on the oxer, and I let him increase his speed just enough to get him over the spread.

I started counting strides in my head. *Three, two, one . . .*

On "one," I rose out of the saddle and Charm leaned back on his haunches, pushing off the dirt ground. Adrenaline kicked in and I loved the feeling of hovering in the air, even for a few seconds, above the ground. Charm landed softly on the other side, his hooves hitting the dirt with barely a sound.

The next vertical, with flower boxes on the sides, was strides away. But Charm was prepared. He moved with ease over the vertical and didn't even glance at the faux flowers. The next vertical and the second oxer, with a wider spread, were no problem for Charm. The daily workouts we had with Mr. Conner kept us both in good shape.

Remembering how Aristocrat had rushed the final jump, and not wanting to make the same mistake, I slowed Charm well before we reached the vertical. I kept my fingers closed around the reins and my legs light against his side, signaling that I wanted him to keep the same speed. Charm responded to my cues and didn't try to yank the reins through my fingers to move faster.

We've got this! I thought, smiling to myself.

We finished our half circle, and I pointed him at the jump. My head snapped up as I saw Callie and Brit. There was no doubt what they were doing—they were battling.

It wasn't a dangerous, pushing-the-limits-with-the-horses type of fight. But Brit and Callie's battle looked like a carefully calculated, well-practiced ballet on horseback.

Omigod! I looked back between Charm's ears, desperate for a clean ride and to get him over the higher vertical. But I knew it was too late. His takeoff was too late and he knocked the poles.

Cringing, I pulled him to a halt—not wanting to look back at Heather. She was going to know *exactly* what had happened.

And she was going to rip me for it.

I swallowed and turned Charm toward Heather. The look on her face was exactly what I'd expected. She had her head cocked, an eyebrow arched, and her eyes were locked on my face.

"Do it again," she said. "Right now. That was ridiculous."

"I know," I said. "I shouldn't have—"

Heather waved her hand. "Stop talking."

I closed my mouth—embarrassment making me sink into the saddle.

"That was worse than a beginner mistake—I don't even know what to call it. You could have hurt Charm or yourself, especially with a jump of that height."

I lowered my head, knowing she was right. The most dangerous time to lose focus was when jumping. I reached down to rub Charm's neck, feeling awful for putting him at risk.

"Don't," Heather said. "The mushy stuff wastes my time. Turn around and do the course again."

"Okay." My face was flushed from Heather's comments, but at least she'd kept her voice low and Callie and Brit couldn't have heard what she said.

I didn't even circle Charm, I directed him back to the course, shook off my nerves, and kept my focus where it should have been in the first place—on my ride. Charm responded to the extra attention. His back became more supple, and the tension I hadn't noticed during our first ride disappeared.

I kept my eyes trained on each jump in front of us, and my own breaths seemed to match Charm's.

We headed for the final jump with no doubt in my brain that we'd clear it. At the right second, Charm pushed up off the ground and launched into the air. This round, our timing was right. He landed cleanly with his back hooves hitting the dirt well away from the jump.

"Good boy," I said. I patted his shoulder, letting him canter for a few more strides before slowing him to a trot and then a walk.

Allowing him to stretch his neck, I gave him a few extra inches of rein. I halted him in front of Heather and she looked at me, not saying anything.

"What?" I asked. "That was way better! You can't say I wasn't focused."

"Omigod, calm down. Did I say you weren't paying attention this time?"

"No," I grumbled.

"Then shut up and listen." Heather half smiled. "That was actually a good ride. When you're only thinking about the next jump and your horse, you're not an awful rider. Your hands did move around too much on landings and you can't plop back in the saddle like you did when Charm landed after the oxer."

I listened, even though it was hard to be critiqued, because I knew if anyone would be right—it would be Heather.

"Charm also did better during this ride. He knew you were paying attention to him, and he didn't try to pull anything. You need to get over being distracted by other riders—it's only going to get worse as we start showing for the YENT."

"You're right," I said. "I know. Charm and I worked so hard to get on the team and I can't mess it up now. Not for anything."

"Good." Heather's tone was serious. "Prove it and run through flatwork with me."

Without another word, we exercised the horses until sweat darkened their coats. Heather and I looked at each other, nodding, and slowed the horses from a working trot to a walk. For forty minutes, I hadn't watched Callie or Brit. Everything Heather had said resonated with me, and I'd kept my concentration on Charm. With the schooling show only days away, I didn't have time to be distracted.

"I'm going to cool him out," Heather said. She dismounted and looked up at me. "You finished?"

"Yeah, we're done. I'm waiting for Brit. We're going on a trail ride."

Heather gave me a lazy wave. "Have fun."

She loosened Aristocrat's girth and led him out of the arena.

Brit turned Apollo in a circle, noticing Heather leaving. She walked her gelding over. "I'm *so* done," she said. "You still up for trail riding?"

"Definitely," I said. "It's time to get out of the arena."

Side-by-side, we let the horses walk toward the exit, leaving Callie and Black Jack alone in the arena.

14

SQUIRREL PHOBIA

IT COULDN'T HAVE BEEN A BETTER TIME TO get away from the stable, campus, and, well, everything. Brit and I were quiet as we walked the horses over the grassy space behind the stable and headed for the woods. With every step Charm took, the anxiety I felt about everything going on lessened. Trail riding was one of my favorite things to do, and I needed it before tomorrow, when Jacob told Callie the truth.

"Callie's a fantastic dressage rider," Brit said, almost as if she could tell that I was thinking about her.

"She's amazing," I said. "She works harder than anyone I know. It was really awful when she didn't make the YENT at our last tryouts."

"Well, the way she just rode, I can't believe she didn't

ELITE AMBITION

make it," Brit said. "What happened?" She shook her head. "Sorry. You don't have to tell me that. I know she used to be your best friend."

"No, it's okay," I said. "It actually feels good to talk about the situation with someone who wasn't around when it happened."

The horses stepped onto the dirt path and I neck-reined Charm, taking in every bit of enjoyment from the ride.

"Callie was the most focused rider *ever*. Probably in, like, school history," I said. "We were almost immediate best friends when I came to Canterwood. But . . ."

Siiigh. I *just* couldn't tell Brit about the Jacob sitch yet. It was too risky before tomorrow.

"But," I continued. "We let a guy get between us and now we're not friends. Callie sort of lost focus on riding, which had been all she'd cared about, and it cost her a spot on the YENT. It was hard to see her go through that."

I flashed back to the moment when Callie had left Mr. Conner's office after he'd told her his decision. Heather and I had been waiting outside the bench, probably both equally nervous to hear the decision. Callie and Heather had never been friends, but Heather knew Callie was a great rider who deserved to make the team despite her mistakes in the days before testing.

"Hey," Brit said, her voice soft. "Sorry. You look so sad. I didn't mean to bring up something that made you upset."

"No, no. It's not that at all. I was just thinking about how Callie handled it when she didn't make the team. At least when she tests this time, she'll know she did every-thing she could—no matter what happens. Last time, she accepted the decision because she didn't think she'd been focused enough."

"That's hard," Brit said. "I went through something kind of like that last year. I crushed on this guy in science class and pretty much obsessed about him every second. Instead of practicing like I should have for a big show, I was going to all of his basketball games and hoping he'd notice me."

"Did he?" I asked.

We both ducked as our horses entered the woods and walked under a low-hanging tree branch.

"I finally went up to him to say hi at one of his games," Brit said. "And he had no clue who I was. He was like, 'Don't we have math together or something?' I was so embarrassed! We'd shared a science textbook before and he didn't even remember."

"*You* shouldn't have been embarrassed," I said. "He should have been for not remembering you." I sighed. "Boys."

Brit and I laughed, letting Charm and Apollo pick their pace as they walked down the dirt path. Both horses seemed content with an easy walk, and Charm bobbed his head as he moved.

"I think they're enjoying the scenery as much as I am," Brit said. "It's gorgeous out here."

"I know—I love it too. There are a zillion trails around here that I can show you."

Brit grinned. "Awesome."

Apollo and Charm started down a slight incline, and Brit and I leaned back in the saddle to keep our balance. The dirt path leveled off after a few yards, and now the trees were so dense around us that I couldn't see any part of campus. I tried to stay relaxed, but my mind kept shifting to Callie and Jacob. There was no way I could predict what was going to happen between them. Part of me wondered if Callie would want to talk to me tomorrow, but the other half felt like she wouldn't, once Jacob told her that he and I were going to try dating.

A squirrel darted onto the path and then tore off into the brush causing a loud rustling. Apollo snorted, yanking on the reins and crabstepping. Brit pushed her heel into his side, but Apollo took another step sideways and caused my boot to bump against Brit's. Caught off guard, I steadied myself in the saddle.

"Sorry!" Brit said. She halted Apollo and rubbed his neck. White showed around the gelding's eyes and his nostrils flared pink.

"Omigosh, don't worry about it," I said. "It happens! He's in a new surrounding, and Charm's spooked *plenty* of times."

Brit took a breath and turned Apollo in a few circles. "Thanks, Sash. I'll keep a better eye on him. Your leg's okay, right?"

I waved my hand. "Totally fine. You barely brushed against me. Let's keep going. The trail gets even better— you'll see."

"Yeah, I don't want to let him think we're going home because of that," Brit said. "He'll calm down again as we keep walking."

We started the horses forward at a walk and the trail widened. I scooted Charm a few inches away from Apollo, giving Brit extra room in case Apollo spooked again.

"He's always been afraid of squirrels," Brit said. "I don't know what happened before I got him, but he has definite squirrel phobia. How long have you had Charm?"

"I got Charm when he was five, and I've had him for about four years. He was supergreen when my parents bought him. During our first few weeks together, I spent more time on the ground on my butt than in the saddle."

Brit grinned. "I've ridden plenty of those horses. But it seems like you guys are bonded now."

"We definitely are," I said. "I swear that he knows what I'm thinking sometimes."

"I feel the same about Apollo. We're usually so in tune—I should have anticipated his reaction to the squirrel—it all just happened so fast. I've only been riding him for about six months, but it feels so much longer than that."

"Six months?" I couldn't keep the shock out of my voice. "Are you serious? You guys look as if you've been practicing together for years."

"Thanks," Brit said, blushing. "I've always ridden stable horses and my parents couldn't afford to buy a horse. We're leasing Apollo from a girl at my old stable who's away at college."

"That's cool that she let you lease him," I said. "So do you get to lease him for as long as you want?"

Brit looked at me, sadness in her dark brown eyes. "Probably only until she graduates. Or, if she decides she wants more money, she could sell him. Our lease was for a year, so I could lose Apollo in six months if she ends our deal then."

I stared at her. "No way. That couldn't happen. You guys are perfect for each other. I'm sure if she ever decided to sell him that you could talk her into letting you keep leasing him. I mean, you made the YENT with him. And who knows, maybe she'll grow out of horses. Some people do when they're in college."

"Not me," Brit said. "My dream is to take Apollo with me wherever I go. I'm crossing my fingers that I can buy him eventually."

I felt for her. It had to be a constant worry if she was going to lose her horse. I'd never had that with Charm.

"I'd keep doing what you are by working hard and proving you both make the best team."

"That's all I can do for right now," Brit said. "I'm grateful every day to have this guy." Apollo bounced, arching his neck as if he understood her. "Oh, don't get a huge ego," Brit told him, laughing.

The trail narrowed and twisted, so we had to ride single file while we talked.

"So we've covered how we got our horses," I said. "What about family? Got any brothers or sisters?"

"Two older sisters," Brit said. "Ainslee's a junior at MIT, and Rachelle's a freshman at CalArts."

"Wow, they're both *so* different. MIT and CalArts—that's awesome. So you've got one sister who's a math genius and one who loves art."

"Rachelle's an amazing painter," Brit said. "She's always wanted to live in California. She almost died when she got accepted."

"I'm awful at math, and I can't even finger paint," I said. "So it'll definitely never be either of those schools for me. I love to read, though. English is my favorite subject."

"I love books too," Brit said. "History's my favorite class. I love my teacher, and I've always liked history as long as I don't have to memorize dates. I've got the worst memory with that!"

"Meee too. I'm awful with dates."

We reached the meadow and had enough room to ride side by side. Apollo seemed much calmer once he was out of the woods and in an open field.

"What about you? Any brothers or sisters?" Brit asked.

"Only child. That's why I never learned how to share," I joked.

Brit laughed. "So *that's* what your problem was when I asked to borrow a dandy brush the other day."

We bantered back and forth as the horses walked. It seemed to only take a couple of minutes for us to reach the fence that separated Canterwood property from a neighboring farm.

"We've got to turn around here," I said. "But we can go back a different way that's out of the woods, mostly, and has a few places to jump. Interested?"

"Um, yeah!" Brit turned Apollo in a circle away from the fence.

"We've got tons of room to canter and let the horses stretch their legs after that workout. Charm doesn't seem tired from the lesson, so I don't think he'll mind a few jumps."

"Same with Apollo. He's good to go."

"Follow me!" I said. Leaning forward in the saddle, I ran my hands along Charm's neck and gave him rein. Charm moved into a smooth canter that carried him with ease over the grass. I could hear Apollo behind us, and I guided Charm to the side of the meadow so he could canter alongside the stone wall. We moved fast past the gray stones with ivy growing over and around them.

Up ahead, I spotted the first of three brush hedges. Apollo's hoofbeats dropped slightly further behind Charm to give us plenty of room. It was common courtesy and safety in case something went wrong. But Charm was ready for the jumps. He cleared the first brush hedge with barely a pause and cantered for the next. We soared over the second jump, and I heard Apollo and Brit land. Charm pulled against the reins, wanting to go faster, but I held him at the same pace. He didn't need to get into a bad habit of always rushing the last jump.

Charm didn't fight me again in the final stride to the hedge. He leaped up and cleared the jump. I knew his hooves didn't even come close to touching the greenery.

We kept cantering, and a few strides later Brit and Apollo were beside us.

"That was great!" Brit said. "It just feels so good to get out of the arena."

"I know. I love practicing and we need to for the show, but we already did that today. Sometimes, I really think taking a little time off helps the horses get focused again."

"And maybe the riders, too," Brit added, smiling.

"Definitely."

I looked ahead, making sure I was thinking of the right path. "Okay, so if we trot for a few yards, we're going to reach the woods. There are a couple of log jumps that Mr. Conner set up and a stream to wade through."

"Apollo loves water," Brit said. "I'm totally game."

We nodded at each other and let the horses trot. Apollo and Charm stayed beside each other until we reached the woods. Brit let Apollo drop back and get behind Charm and me.

Charm kept the same smooth pace as he entered the woods and didn't shy at any of the kind of scary-looking shadows the trees cast along the path. I gave him more rein and he bounced forward into a canter. But I didn't let him go too fast—not in the woods. We stayed at a slow pace, reaching the first of two log jumps. These types of jumps always made me a little nervous because they were solid. If I made a mistake and let Charm take off at the wrong time, he could be seriously injured if he hit a log.

But I wasn't going to think about that. If I got nervous, so would Charm. Staying loose in the saddle, I moved with him and let him head for the log. The giant object loomed before us.

You've done this a zillion times! I told myself.

I started counting strides to distract myself from worrying. *Five, four, three, two, one, now!*

On my silent "now," Charm lifted into the air and

tucked his knees under his body. The second he left the ground, I knew he would clear the log. His timing had been perfect and he'd had the right amount of speed to get over the jump. The log flashed under us and Charm landed on the other side. We kept cantering, and, seconds later, I heard Apollo land behind us. Charm and I cantered around a bend in the trail and the path started to curve. The next log wasn't as immediately visible as the first.

We rounded a corner, and I spotted the log only strides ahead of us. A soft breeze blew back Charm's mane as he cantered for the log, not even hesitating. And that was part of the reason I loved Charm—he was a fearless jumper and he trusted me enough to get him over any obstacle.

Leaves and branches swept by my face as we neared the log. At what felt like the right second, I eased my hands along his neck and lifted out of the saddle. Charm pushed off with his hind legs and launched over the log. If Mr. Conner could see this I was certain he'd give Charm's form a ten.

We landed and I pulled him to a trot, easing him to the side of the trail while we waited for Brit and Apollo. It took them only seconds to reach us, and Brit's excitement was all over her face.

"*That* was amazing," she said. "I love jumping logs—the adrenaline is insane. This is a great course!"

"Isn't it awesome?" I asked. "I love it. And it's good for Charm too, to get used to moving from an open field to the woods. He needs the challenge of moving fast then having to adjust to a slower pace when I want him to."

"Good point," Brit said. "The horses do have to acclimate to the lighting, the pacing, like you said, and the different footing."

We eased the horses to walks since we were nearing the end of the ride and neither of us wanted barn sour horses. The stream I'd told Brit about appeared and, just like Brit had said, Apollo stepped right in. Charm followed beside him and both horses seemed to enjoy the coolness of the water against their legs after our lesson and trail ride. I remembered how Charm used to be afraid of water and how Callie had helped me get him past it.

I let the reins dangle from one hand, relaxing in the saddle. Brit kicked her feet out of the stirrups and let Apollo move at a lazy walk.

"What are you doing after this?" Brit asked.

"After Charm's taken care of, I'm going back to my room to attack the mountain of homework that's waiting for me. What about you?"

"Same, unfortunately. Want to come back to my room to do homework?"

"Well, I . . ." I paused. I was hoping Paige would be in our room so we could finally talk about the Callie thing, but even if that didn't come up I wanted to hang out with her. *But* she had mentioned that she was hoping to see Geena—and I had to believe she meant *Geena*—after she did her own homework.

"Let me text my roommate when we get back," I said. "If she's not in our room, it would be great to do homework together."

"Cool," Brit said.

We finished the walk back and I found my phone in my tack trunk.

R u doing hmwk in r room? I texted Paige.

Nope, decided 2 go 2 Geena's.

OK—gonna go 2 Brit's 4 hmwk and c u back in r room aftr.

K! ☺

I put away my phone and called down the aisle to Brit, who had Apollo in crossties. "My roommate's going to be out for a while," I said. "So, if it's still cool, I'd love to do homework at your place."

"Of course it's still cool. I know you have to get your stuff, but we can head out together if you want."

"Definitely."

I grabbed the dandy brush to brush off dirt that clung to Charm's legs from the trail ride. It took me a little longer to get his sock clean, but when it was pure white again, I went back to the rest of his coat. It didn't take much to make his chestnut coat glossy, and he blinked sleepily as I brushed him with a softer body brush. If I allowed him to eat while I groomed him, he'd let me brush him all day. But food was his top priority.

I finished grooming him, mucked his stall, and gave him a flake of hay. His water bucket was full, so he was set for the night.

"Okay, boy," I said. "I had so much fun with you today. You were perfect, and I'm so proud of you."

Charm let me kiss his muzzle, then I turned him loose in his stall. Like always, he went straight for his hay net and had torn a mouthful of hay from the flake before I'd even left the stall.

I shook my head, laughing, and gathered his tack. Brit and I ran into each other in the tack room, and we put away our horses' stuff. We left the stable and headed for our dorms.

"I'll grab my homework, change, and meet you at your room," I said.

"Cool. See you in a few."

15

STRANGERS

BACK IN MY ROOM, I GATHERED UP MY BOOKS and papers, shoving them into my backpack. I was disappointed that Paige wasn't here so we could talk. But I was also excited to see Brit's room. I couldn't even imagine what her space looked like, and I was curious.

I changed from my riding clothes into jeans, a fave pink v-neck shirt, and a black jacket dotted with tiny rhinestones.

I left Winchester, heading across campus to Orchard.

"Sasha, hey," Julia said. We met just as I opened the door. "What're you doing here?"

"Homework with Brit," I said. There was a flicker of annoyance on Julia's face. "What about you? Where are you going?"

"To meet Ben," Julia said. "We're going to see a movie."

"Fun. Hope it's a good flick. See you later."

I stepped around her, heading for Brit's room.

"Sasha?"

I turned back to Julia. "Yeah?"

Julia stepped back inside and let the door close behind her. "Are you and Brit, like, best friends now?"

"Brit and I are *friends*. We haven't known each other long enough to be best friends," I said.

Julia stared me down. "Fine. Just remember that you're also spending a lot of time with us."

"And?" I shook my head.

"*And* even though Heather and Alison like Brit and seem all about making her part of the Trio, I don't trust her, so don't go spilling any of our business to her that you hear."

"Why don't you trust Brit?" I asked. "You've barely spoken to her."

Julia adjusted the shoulder strap on her purse. "I don't know. Maybe I'm being paranoid or whatever, but there's something off about her. And I don't want anyone else in our group. Especially when we're still adjusting to *you*."

"Wow, thanks," I said, sarcasm in my voice. "I don't know what your deal is with Brit, but you've got to be kidding that *I'm* part of the Trio. That's insane. I hang out with you guys, but it's not like Heather put me through an initiation or something. She never informed you and Alison that the Trio was becoming a 'Quartet.' You really need to chill."

Julia opened her mouth, looking ready to fight back, but instead turned and shoved open the door. It shuddered behind her—its angry sound echoing through the hallway.

I shook off my annoyance with Julia. It wasn't worth it, and I had too many other things on my mind to worry about besides one-third of the Trio.

I wandered down the hallway, taking in the cranberry-colored walls and enjoying getting out of Winchester. It was fun to be in a different dorm, and I'd always loved the color scheme and feel of Orchard. I found Brit's room and knocked on the door. Unlike the last time I'd seen it, her door had been decorated. She'd put up a purple, glittery "B" near the top of the door, and she'd taped pictures of people who looked like they'd be her parents and sisters under the B. There were also photos of Apollo. I spotted my favorite one immediately—it was an early morning photo where the sun was rising over the back of a pasture. Dew glinted off the grass, and Apollo was looking right into the camera. His gray face looked so gentle—I almost wanted to pet the photo.

I smiled at the pic, then knocked on Brit's door.

"Hey," Brit said, pulling open the door. "C'mon in!"

She'd changed into cozy gray yoga pants, a pocket T-shirt, and a hoodie.

"Hope you like my room," she said, gesturing with one hand.

I stepped inside, putting my backpack on glossy hardwood floor. Brit's room was a few feet bigger than mine and Paige's. One bed was made with a lilac and white striped comforter. The other, empty, had a neat stack of laundry on it. A giant whiteboard on the wall had scribbles with neon-colored markers that had notes like *hist extra credit due 2mrw* and *I <3 Todd on DVD nxt month.*

Her closet doors were closed and a few pairs of sneakers were tossed in a pile beside the door. A thick pink area rug covered most of the floor, leaving only a few feet of hardwood near the walls. The bathroom door was closed and next to the door was a glass desk with a black swivel chair.

Between the two beds, Brit had a black lamp table with shelves under it that were stacked with books, a few glass horse figurines and a bonsai tree. The clear lamp was chic and modern. Brit had twinkly lights shaped like tiny stars draped along the wall across the space between the windows. I bet the lights cast fun shadows at night.

"I love your curtains," I said, walking over to one of the two windows to check out the view.

"Thanks—I found them at Pottery Barn Teen. I'm totally obsessed with that store!"

The off-white eyelet lace curtains flowed from clear curtain rods with a shiny acrylic star at the ends of each rod. I pulled back a curtain, and looked out the window from Brit's second story double. This window faced the gym—a place I'd yet to visit—and the outdoor pool.

"Your room is awesome!" I said. "I'd decorate *exactly* the same way."

"Then we both *obviously* have good taste," Brit said, grinning. "I'm glad you like it."

"It must be nice to have a room to yourself sometimes," I said. "Or are you ready for a roommate now?"

"I'm pretty social," Brit said. "I hope I get assigned a roommate soon."

"I'm sure you will. Doubles don't have just one person in them for long. Especially if you really want a roomie."

"Fingers crossed," Brit said. She glanced toward her desk, sighing. "Shall we?"

"I guess we should," I said. "If we don't get started soon, I'll never finish everything before tomorrow."

"Want to grab snacks first?" Brit asked. "I think we could probably use a little caffeine and something of the sugar variety."

"Most definitely," I said.

Brit and I went to Orchard's spacious common room and looked through the kitchen cabinets for what we wanted.

I grabbed a snack-sized bag of Cooler Ranch Doritos, a box of gummy worms, and a can of root beer.

"What'd you get?" I asked, looking over at Brit.

"Sprite, M&M's, and chips," she said. "All of the essentials."

She grinned at my snack choices, and we walked toward the door.

"I love Orchard's common room," I said. "It's alw—" I closed my mouth when the door pushed open.

Callie stood there.

Her long black hair was loose around her shoulders. She'd dusted shimmery eyeshadow on her eyelids that made her brown eyes look even darker. I waited, frozen, for a look of fury or *something* from her. But she looked at me as if we were strangers. Everything about her—from her jeans and slouch boots to her butterfly earrings—reminded me of my former best friend. Everything except the way she was looking at me now.

Brit, standing beside me, shifted her snacks into the crook of her left arm.

"Hi, we haven't met yet," Brit said. "I think I heard around the stable that you're Callie, right?"

Callie looked at Brit. "Yeah, hi. I'm Callie." Her tone wasn't friendly or chilly—just without emotion. "Brit?"

Brit nodded, sticking out her right hand. "Yep—new girl at school."

Brit's tone was light and without any hint that she knew any of my history with Callie.

Callie nodded, stepping around us without looking at me. "Welcome to Canterwood. I'm sure I'll be seeing you around."

I started to turn around and ask Callie if she'd talk to me. For a second, I considered not waiting for Jacob to tell her the truth.

"Ready?" Brit asked.

I stared at her—unable to make a decision.

"Ready," I said, finally, after too many seconds passed.

I followed Brit out of the common room and down the hallway.

"Thanks for the save," I said, able to form words now that we were away from the common room.

"No problem," Brit said. "Situations like that are so awkward, but I would have done the same thing. Don't even worry about it."

Brit opened the door to her room, and before I took a step inside, I forced myself to shake off the Callie encounter.

Two hours later, Brit and I groaned and stretched simultaneously.

"I. Quit," I said.

"Me. Too," Brit said in the same tone.

I flipped my science textbook shut and dropped it below me. I was sitting in Brit's pod chair near her floor lamp. She was at her desk, and we'd been working non-stop since we'd gotten snacks.

"If I read one more page, my brain's going to explode," I said. "All of the root beer in the common room can't save me."

Brit nodded. "Same here. I've been stuck on the same math problem for twenty minutes. I'll have to ask my teacher for help tomorrow."

"Want me to look at it?" I asked. "I'm not the *best* at math, but I could try."

"You sure?" Brit held out her notebook to me. "It's problem twenty-nine—the last one."

I read the problem, staring at her bubbly handwriting. "Okay, it's possible that I'm delusional, but I think I know how to solve this."

"Really?"

I got up off the chair and flopped onto Brit's bed with a pen and the notebook. Brit got beside me, and I walked her through the problem.

"So, after we move the negative two over here, then we're set to solve the equation," I said. "Can you do the next line?"

Brit stared at the paper, her pen hovering over the problem. But she bent over it and scribbled in the next line of the equation.

"Is that totally wrong?" she asked, wincing.

I read through her work twice, shaking my head. "Nope! You got it. Now just do the next line and solve it. Then we're really done."

"Okay, one sec."

I packed up my books and let Brit focus on her problem. I checked my phone for texts and there was one from Paige.

Back in r room. Hmwk done—gag. Ready 2 chill when u get back.

Leaving v soon! I sent the text.

"And . . . done!" Brit said. She closed her math book—there was visible relief on her face. "Thank you so much."

"I'm glad I could help," I said. "Don't ever worry about asking a teacher or me or someone if you need help. It's only your first week here, and you're waaay more put together than I was, like, two months after being here."

Brit looked at her math book, then up at me. "Thanks. And I *really* doubt that's true, only because it seems like you've been a student here forever. It's so dumb, but I feel embarrassed to ask teachers or people I don't know for help. This school is so tough—I don't want anyone to think I can't handle it."

"No one would think that. Ever," I said. "You'd get more respect if you asked for help with whatever than if you faked your way through it."

Brit nodded, twirling her pen.

"And besides," I said. "You're the one who just got here over the weekend and acts as if she's been here for years. You're outgoing, friendly, and everyone—even the Trio—wants you to be part of their group."

"The Trio's really interested in me?" Brit asked, her head tilted as if she didn't believe me.

"Honestly? Alison adores you. Julia's wary with everyone,

and Heather wants you in her group. Pause to take note that she *never* does that."

Brit shook her head, laughing quietly. "They're all cool girls, well, except for Julia 'cause she kind of hates me. But what if I don't want to be part of anyone's group? I just got here, and I'd rather have friends—like all of you guys—than jump into a clique or something."

I nodded at Brit. "Got to say that I'm impressed. Most girls would have done *anything* to be Heather's friend and to get into the Trio."

Brit rolled her eyes. "I saw enough of that at my old school. Cliques were rampant, and it was never something I was into. I'd rather be popular, or not, on my own."

"I've bounced around among friends since I got here," I said. "Paige is my best friend and before the mess with Jacob, Callie and I were also best friends. How lucky can a girl get to have *two* best friends?"

Brit nodded, but didn't interrupt me.

"And that was when the Trio was torturing me. Then, things fell apart between Callie and me, and the more I talked to Heather, the more I liked her. It sounds crazy to even say that now. But Alison and I got closer, much to Julia's dismay, and now we're all sort of friends. I'm definitely *not* part of their group, but we're friends."

"Do you want to be part of the Trio?" Brit asked.

I paused. "I don't know. I kind of like things the way they are right now—with me on the outside. Like you, I'm not all about being popular or cliquey, but I also can't say that I'm sorry the Trio's decided to stop torturing me."

"Please, as if I'd complain about that either," Brit said. "Just because you're friends with them doesn't mean you have to join their group—unless you want to."

Brit started picking up her textbooks, and I slung my bag over my shoulder. "Thanks for letting me hang out today," I said. "Even though we were doing homework, I still had lots of fun."

"Me too," Brit said, smiling. "And next time we'll do it at your place. I'd love to see your dorm."

"For sure. And thanks again for being so cool with Callie."

"Seriously, it was no big deal."

We smiled at each other, and I left Orchard thinking about how Brit had no idea how big a deal her help *really* had been.

When I got back to my room, Paige was in her pj's lying on top of her bed reading *The Secret Garden*.

"I thought you were done studying," I said.

Paige nodded, holding up her copy of *The Secret Garden* full of sticky notes. "I'm not really studying, just reading. I figured I needed a head start. I'm only going to get *more* homework over the weekend, and this class is important to me."

"Good point," I said. "I wish I had your will to study, but I can't. I'm changing and going to sleep."

Paige closed her book, yawning. "I'm doing the same. I want to read more, but I'm too tired."

I sensed *something* was off with Paige, but I didn't know what. I grabbed a clean pair of pajamas—black Hello Kitty shorts and a white T-shirt—and headed to the bathroom to change and get ready for bed.

When I came out, Paige's light was out, and she looked half-asleep already. I was exhausted and didn't want to start a fight, but I couldn't hold it in any longer. I couldn't wait for Paige to come to me about Callie.

"So, um, Brit and I went to The Sweet Shoppe yesterday," I said.

"Oh, what'd you get?" Paige asked.

"Ice cream sundaes." I stopped, feeling unsure about how to approach her with this. But I knew I had to.

"That sounds so good," Paige said. "Yum."

"It was good. But I wanted to talk to you about The Sweet Shoppe. I saw you there with Callie."

Paige started to sit up in bed, a look of alarm on her face.

"No, no, I don't care," I said, getting under my covers. "I know you guys were friends before this whole mess started. Even though Callie and I aren't friends anymore, it doesn't mean that you can't be."

Paige dipped her head. "I know you don't care. That was a dumb thing to do. I should have told you I was having dessert with her instead of lying about it."

"You were probably worried that it would make me feel uncomfortable," I said. "And it doesn't—I promise. I'm glad you guys are still friends. But you know you can tell me the truth about whom you're going out with even if it is Callie."

Paige nodded. "I'll definitely be honest with you about it from now on. Promise."

"None of what happened was Callie's fault. She probably needs all the friends and support she can get right now."

Paige yawned. "Definitely. 'Night."

I flicked off my lamp. "'Night."

I stared at the ceiling for a long time trying to fall

asleep. Something wasn't right. Paige hadn't done anything wrong, and I believed that she'd tell me the truth if she was going to meet Callie, but I still felt that something was off. I just didn't know what.

16

OKAYISH

ON FRIDAY MORNING, I WASN'T SURE IF I WAS going to go to classes or not. Almost all night, I'd thought of a dozen excuses I could give Livvie that would convince her to let me take the day off. Just thinking about Jacob telling Callie the truth made me dizzy. It felt like my chest was being crushed with that, classes, and the show on Sunday. A show Callie and I would both be attending.

I grabbed my phone and texted Jacob. *When r u telling C?*

He wrote back almost immediately. *Aftr class. U ok?*

I paused, but didn't want to take too long or he'd think something was up.

Okayish.

Hope 2 run into u 2day b4 I talk 2 Callie. I want u 2 feel good with this decision 2.

Yeah, hope 2 see u soon 2.

And that's when I decided I was going to class. If I stayed in bed all day, I'd just worry and make myself crazy. I needed the distraction of other people. So I climbed out of bed, got dressed, and followed Paige out the door.

Luckily for me, English class was a review for Monday's test. There was no assigned homework.

"Finally," Paige said. "At least we know *one* class doesn't have homework even though we'll be studying all weekend for the test."

"I know," I said. "I mean, studying *is* lots of work, but we both have tons of notes, and I know we'll get good grades on it."

"Always," Paige said.

"See you later?"

"I'll see you later," Paige replied as we reached the stairwell.

Almost in a daze, I hurried down the stairs, not even paying attention to where I was walking.

"Sash."

I looked up and Jacob stood a step below me, smiling.

"Hey."

"I only have a few minutes before my next class," I said. "But can we talk for a sec?"

"Of course."

Jacob and I stood on the landing at the bottom of the stairwell. No one was coming up or down, at least not yet, but I kept my eyes on the doors.

"Jacob, I want us to try being together. I *really* do. And I want Callie to know the truth, even though I know it'll hurt her. She does deserve to know. But if I'm being totally selfish? I'm stressing so much about you telling her today. I'm worried that it'll throw off the show for her—and for me—to have something like that dropped on her this close to our show."

Jacob took a breath. "There's never going to be a right time to do this," he said. "But I see your point. I'm willing to wait, but only until Sunday when you all come back and the show's over."

"Really?" Anxiety flooded out of my body and I almost dropped my backpack. "You *sure*?"

"Totally sure," Jacob said. "It's your first show for the YENT, and Callie's riding in another division, I think. So there's no way I want to mess that up for either of you."

The door above us opened, and I stepped back from Jacob. "Okay," I said. "Sounds like a plan." I didn't want to say too much and give us away.

We hurried in opposite directions, and I didn't dare

glance back at him. At the bottom of the stairwell, I pushed open the door and exited the building. Once I got outside, I took in a gulp of fresh air. I knew this was *not* news Callie needed before she attended a show. And I was lucky that Jacob understood that, even though it meant he had to wait longer to tell the truth. A couple of extra days felt like nothing after how long we'd been hiding the truth to protect Callie's feelings.

17

JUMP-OFF

I PRACTICALLY SKIPPED TO RIDING PRACTICE after my conversation with Jacob. I knew Jacob would still have to tell Callie, but at least it wasn't happening *today*. And for now, I could focus on practicing for the show. I walked down the stable aisle, and Heather darted out of Aristocrat's stall.

"Guess who's in a meeting in Mr. Conner's office?" I asked.

"Who?"

I kept walking toward the tack room with Heather following me.

"Mr. Conner asked Julia, Alison, and Callie into his office," Heather said.

"For what?"

Heather and I gathered our horses' tack into our arms.

"YENT tryouts," Heather said.

"Ohhhh. Whoa. I knew that was coming. When do you think it is?"

"No clue," Heather said. "Soon, I assume."

We walked back down the aisle, and I paused by Aristocrat's stall. "It's going to be interesting," I said.

"They're all going to fight for it—you know that," Heather said. "I told Julia and Alison not to slow at practice for a second because I watched Callie and she was *good*."

"She is good," I said. "But Julia and Alison can hold their own."

Heather put Aristocrat's tack on the trunk outside his stall. "It's really anybody's seat, but I think Julia and Alison are already feeling defeated. And they can't go into it with that attitude."

"Agreed. Or they're giving up before they've even started."

Heather looked at me, almost as if she was studying me. "You know, you used to talk a lot and I never listened to you. I still don't, most of the time, but that was actually good."

"Wow, thanks a lot," I said. "I'm glad to hear it."

I half rolled my eyes at her and walked away. Just as I was stepping away from Aristocrat's stall, Julia and Alison hurried over to Heather.

"Omigod!" they both said at the same time.

"What?" Heather asked.

I stopped, looking at both of them.

"Testing's next week," Julia said. "We test next week. I can't even believe it."

"That's great," Heather said. She led Aristocrat out of his stall and tied him to the iron bars in front of his stall. "It'll give you just enough time to fine-tune things, but not too much time to get crazy nervous."

Julia and Alison both blew out a giant breath at the same time.

"True," Alison said, wiping a wisp of hair out of her face. "At first, I was like, 'Omigod! That's way too soon.' But you're right. I'd rather test and just know."

"You'll both do great," I said. "You would have been ready the first time if Jasmine hadn't gotten in the way."

"Thanks," Alison said. She rubbed her palms on her chocolate-colored breeches. "It's really crunch time now." She and Julia started talking about their practice plans and how they were going to not only ride more, but also watch DVDs and clips online of shows for examples.

I smiled at The Trio, leaving them to plan their YENT strategy, and headed for Charm's stall.

All I could think about was the reality of the situation. Three talented riders were up for *one* slot on the YENT. Two of them weren't going to make it. In my gut, I knew Callie deserved it, but I also liked Alison and Julia, even though Julia was snotty to me sometimes. They were all dedicated riders. I'd feel bad for whoever didn't make it.

"Hey, mister," I said when I reached Charm's stall. "How's it going?"

Charm nickered at me, so softly it was barely audible. I opened his stall door and wrapped my arms around him. He smelled like sweet hay and grain. I reached under his chin and clipped his leather lead line to the ring under his halter.

I led him into the aisle, finding a free pair of cross-ties at the end of the stable.

I clipped him into the crossties and grabbed his tack box, moving it closer to him. Grooming Charm was one of my favorite things to do—it made me feel closer him. I started by picking his hooves, then switched to a body brush. His coat was clean enough that he didn't need the stiffer bristles of the dandy brush. Pieces of hay clung to the underside of his belly, and I swiped them off with the brush.

After I groomed him, I placed his saddle pad on top of his back and smoothed the quilted white pad. I placed his saddle gently on top of his back and did something I hadn't in a while—I inspected his saddle. I checked the stirrup leathers for wear, made sure none of the buckles for his girth showed any signs of stress and looked at the rubber inserts in the stirrup irons to make sure the grips weren't worn down.

"Everything looks good, boy," I said. "I still have to clean all of your tack before the show, but at least I know it's safe."

I took off his halter and placed the reins over his head. I bridled him easily and inspected his bridle just as I had his saddle. Nothing was worn, and we were set to ride.

I led him back to his stall, grabbing my helmet from my trunk. After snapping it on, I led Charm to the indoor arena.

Brit and Heather, already inside, were riding side by side and giggling. They smiled at me when I led Charm inside and mounted. I rode him up to them and eased him into a trot to join them.

"We were just talking about how we are *so* over Katie James," Brit said. "Her last *six* movies have been romantic comedy flops. It's ridiculous."

"The girl needs an acting class, seriously," Heather said, shaking her head. "She just keeps getting cast because her dad's some big Hollywood producer."

"Ugh, that's so gross," I said. "I didn't know that about her dad. Lame."

"Very," Brit said, nodding.

We rode the horses side by side at a posting trot, then let them into canters. Charm shook out his mane and moved next to Apollo. The two horses had already become friends, and Charm didn't seem to be as competitive with Apollo as he was with Aristocrat. Maybe that was an old habit that would never go away.

Mr. Conner walked into the arena, nodding at us. "Good afternoon, girls," he said. "I hope you're all ready to get to work. This will be the last practice before the show. Saturday, you're more than welcome to practice on your own, but if you think you and your horse need a break, then take it. Don't push yourself too hard for the first show of the season."

We nodded at him.

"If everyone's horses are warmed up, then we're going to work on show jumping today," Mr. Conner said. "I've designed a course of five jumps that you're going to ride once forward and then turn around and take in the opposite direction. All of the jumps are verticals—they just vary in height and spacing. I want you to treat this as a jump-off and give a clean, but fast ride as if you're racing the clock. Brit, I'd like you to go first."

Brit didn't waste any time. She heeled Apollo forward and the gelding's wavy gray tail floated behind him as they made their way to the first jump.

Brit rose in the saddle at the right moment, moving her hands up along Apollo's neck. They landed, his hooves not even coming close to touching the rail, and Brit kept him at a fast canter. Within seconds, they'd cleared the second, third, and fourth verticals. I couldn't look away, I didn't even want to blink—afraid I'd miss something. There was more room between the four and fifth jump, so Brit let Apollo increase his speed a notch more. The gelding flew forward and tucked his legs under his body as he cleared the highest vertical.

I cheered in my head. That had been a gorgeous ride. Brit turned Apollo in a wide circle, and they took the course backward. Again, she kept him at a canter that neared a slow gallop, and both horse and rider had beautiful form.

After the last jump, Brit slowed Apollo and rode him back to us. There was a tiny smile on her face.

"Excellent," Mr. Conner said. "You kept up a great pace, but didn't rush him. I'm quite impressed."

Brit blushed. "Thank you," she said.

"Heather," Mr. Conner said. "You may go."

Heather seemed to be fueled by Mr. Conner's comments to Brit. She let Aristocrat leap into a slow gallop toward the first fence, slowing him just before they got too close. In between each jump, she somehow managed to keep him at a canter that verged on a gallop without coming close to touching a rail. When she turned around to take the course in the opposite direction, I couldn't believe what I'd seen. I'd thought Brit's ride had been perfect—impossible to beat. But had it been a real jump-off, Heather would have won.

Heather rode Aristocrat over, not even bothering to hide the cocky smirk on her face.

"That was a daring ride," Mr. Conner said. "Aristocrat was moving so fast that he could have knocked one or all of the jumps. You took a huge risk, but it paid off. That's what jump-offs are about. Being safe is always a top priority, but racing against the clock while riding clean is what you need to win."

Heather almost glowed from the compliment. She and Aristocrat were so in tune, she probably could have taken him at a slow gallop over the course and he would have made it.

Mr. Conner looked at me. "Sasha, whenever you're ready."

I trotted Charm away from the group, then let him in a fast canter. There was no way I'd let him even approach a gallop—not with the way he'd been rushing the last jump lately. We'd have to do our best at this pace.

We flew over the first and second verticals and Charm landed without a pause before he tore off for the third. For a second, I panicked, thinking he'd taken off too late and would drag the rail down with his back hooves. But he somehow managed to clear the rail. I slowed him a fraction before we reached the fourth vertical, and he listened to my cues. He jumped the final two jumps with ease before I turned him back around to take the course again.

We completed it with a clean ride and, grinning, I rode back to the group.

"I'm impressed, Sasha," Mr. Conner said. "I know you probably felt pressure from the imaginary clock, but you know Charm and his habits. He would have rushed the jump and probably taken it down. You made the right call by keeping him a slower pace. I'm proud of your decision."

"Thank you," I said. I patted Charm's neck and he bowed it, proud of his performance.

"Let's run through a few flatwork exercises and then you can cool your horses," Mr. Conner said. "Everyone please move out to the wall."

And for the next half hour, Brit, Heather, and I worked as a team to sharpen our YENT skills.

18

CONFIDENT, NOT COCKY

"WHEEEW," BRIT SAID. "*THAT* WAS INTENSE."

"No kidding," I agreed. We led two tired horses beside us. "Mr. Conner is always focused before a show, but that was a crazy practice session."

"Are you taking tomorrow off?" Brit asked. "Or are you practicing?"

"I'm going to do a light workout with Charm, but nothing too stressful. He needs to be rested before the show."

"I was thinking the same about Apollo," Brit said, she smiled. "And, it sounds so wimpy, but I'm glad for the break too!"

"It's *not* wimpy!" We both laughed. "I'm going to need a break tomorrow too, trust me. You are definitely not the only one."

We led the horses in slow circles along one of the quiet lanes by the side of the stable.

"How are things with Paige?" Brit asked.

I sighed. "Weird. There's definitely tension about Callie, and even though I told her I'm glad they're still friends, I still feel like she's going behind my back to see Callie. It's so unnecessary." I blew out a breath—frustrated. "It's just hard. Paige and I used to be super-tight, and we told each other everything. Things have really changed a lot this semester."

Brit nodded. "I know what you mean. I had the same best friend from kindergarten until sixth grade. We could have been sisters—we were that close. Then, she fell in with the popular crowd in middle school and I didn't. I didn't care about being popular. But she did. She started ditching me to hang out with her new friend and after a while, she didn't even text me back."

"Wow," I said. "I'm sorry. That's awful."

"It was," Brit said. She rubbed Apollo's neck as we walked. "But it also showed me that I never wanted to be one of those girls who was in a clique or thought she was above everyone else."

"Honestly?" I said. "When you first came here, I thought you were probably the most popular girl at your school. I was sure you'd join Heather and her friends. Or act like Jasmine—this awful girl who transferred here and made everyone miserable."

Brit burst into laughter. "Are you serious? You thought *I* was going to be a crazy popular girl who ran Canterwood?"

"Only until I got to know you," I said. "Then I realized you're not cocky and you don't think you're better than everyone else. You're confident. I wish I had more of that."

Brit and I walked in silence for a few seconds, listening to the even sound of our horses' hoofbeats over the grass.

Brit looked at me, her expression serious. "You don't give yourself enough credit for how good of a rider you are. If you saw yourself in the arena, you'd be walking around with what 'confidence' you think I have. You're a great rider, Sash, and it doesn't matter if you're on the YENT, at Canterwood, Briar Creek, or any other stable— you'd still be just as good. I'd bet you that the talent was always there and it just needed to be drawn out."

I kept walking, unsure what to say. "Thank you," I finally managed. "That really means a lot, especially right before a show. I know we're on the same team, but you didn't have to say any of that."

Brit shook her head, smiling. "I wasn't saying it as a teammate. I was saying it as your friend."

We smiled at each other, turning the horses back toward the stable.

"And if you ever want to talk about the Paige sitch," Brit said. "I'm here to listen. If things don't get better and you can't deal, it would be so much fun to be roommates."

"Thanks so much," I said. "For both offers. I'll definitely talk to you about Paige if things don't get better, but I know we're going to work it out. But you're supercool for offering to be my roommate."

The horses' shoes clinked as they hit the aisle, and we walked them to crossties. We couldn't find a pair together and, just this once, I was glad. I untacked Charm and started grooming him on autopilot. I couldn't even believe it, but I was thinking about Brit's offer. I knew I'd never move out of Winchester and leave Paige, but right now, living with Brit sounded tempting.

19

GUEST STARRING AT
LUNCH . . .

ON SATURDAY, I CROSSED THE COURTYARD, heading for the stable. I knew it was going to be packed today with everyone who was attending the show wanting to get in a last-minute practice session.

My phone buzzed, and I pulled it out of my jacket pocket.

Ur prob already @ stable but g luck w ur practice

Jacob's text made me smile.

Thx! Hope u have a fun Sat.

I put my phone back in my pocket took in a breath of fresh air. Two *major* things were happening tomorrow, but I could only focus on one at a time. And first up? The show. The weather was perfect today, and Brit and I had texted and agreed to meet in the big outdoor arena at ten. We planned on having a light practice, then going for lunch. I still didn't know what class she was showing in. Mr. Conner had restricted us to one, since it was our first show of the season. I'd already decided on show jumping.

It didn't take long for me to groom and tack up Charm. I led him down the aisle, weaving around the other horses and students. We got outside and I mounted, letting him move at a springy walk toward the arena.

"Just an easy practice today, boy," I said. "We both have to rest up for tomorrow."

Charm snorted like he agreed, and we reached the arena. Brit was walking Apollo in slow circles.

"Hey!" she called, heading for us.

"Hey," I said back. "Final chance before the show. You ready?"

Brit nodded and patted Apollo's shoulder. "So ready. I was planning on riding for about forty-five minutes— that seems long enough."

"Agreed," I said. "I'm not pushing Charm either. I'm just going to run him through a bunch of flatwork exercises to loosen him up."

"Same."

Brit and I moved our horses to opposite ends of the

arena. I hid a smile when I watched an intermediate rider move his horse far out of the way from Charm and me. *That used to be you,* I thought. It had taken me forever to adjust to saying I was on Canterwood Crest's advanced riding team. Now, I had to almost force out the words "I'm a rider for the YENT." It seemed surreal.

I started Charm with figure eights at a walk, then a trot. I let the pattern get bigger and moved him into a canter. With each completion of the exercise, I felt his muscles loosen. After a few more rounds of figure eights, we did serpentines. Looking down at the opposite end of the arena, I watched Brit work Apollo at a collected trot. The gray gelding had his head down and his legs moved with precision. I squinted, focusing on his left foreleg. For a second I thought he'd favored it. I kept watching, waiting for any warning signs, but he didn't take a misstep or act at all like his hoof was sore.

Satisfied, I focused my attention back on Charm and asked him to halt. My lower back felt tight, so I did a few twists in the saddle, then reached down to touch my toes. Charm stood still as I worked out my body.

After a few more stretches I asked Charm for an extended walk around the length of the arena. I let him trot, relaxed, and noticed the arena was starting to fill up with other horses and riders. I slowed Charm to a walk, reaching down to feel his neck and shoulders. He felt warm and loose.

I looked over at Brit, waiting for her to look in my direction. She did, and I pointed to the exit. Nodding, she trotted Apollo over, and we left the arena together.

"That was perfect," she said. "Just enough."

"I agree," I said. "There's nothing else we can improve between now and tomorrow morning. We're as ready as we're going to be."

We cooled and groomed the horses, then mucked their stalls and gave them fresh hay and water.

I kept Charm on the crossties and pulled out the clippers from his tack trunk. He wasn't spooked by the seminoisy clippers, so I didn't need help holding him. Loosening his halter, I slid it down his neck so his bridle path was clear. I plugged in the red clippers and turned them on. They whirred as I ran them up and down Charm's bridle path until it was smooth and neat.

I changed the blade and carefully ran the clippers over Charm's muzzle until his long chin hairs were gone. He blinked at me, sleepy, as I got him ready for tomorrow.

"You couldn't enjoy this just a bit more, huh?" I teased.

After his bridle path, chin, ears, and fetlocks were trimmed, I turned him loose in his stall.

Charm took a not-so-dainty slurp of water, dribbling everywhere. I laughed, watching him from outside the stall.

"Get a good night's sleep, boy," I said. "Love you and see you in the morning."

I picked up his tack and walked to the tack room. Brit was inside, sitting on a saddle pad and cleaning Apollo's bridle.

I grabbed a sponge and went to work on Charm's tack.

"Is it weird that I actually like cleaning tack?" Brit asked.

"No way," I said. "I don't mind it either. It's probably because we're doing it for our horses and we want them to look and feel good."

"Definitely," Brit said. "Agreed."

We cleaned our tack regularly, so after soaping our bridles and saddles, we buffed them to a soft sheen.

"Nice work," Brit said, high-fiving me as we put on our saddle covers and hung up our bridles.

"I think we deserve dessert with lunch, don't you?" I asked as we headed out.

"Um, most definitely," Brit said.

We walked to The Sweet Shoppe and washed up in the bathroom. At the counter, I ordered a corn dog and fries while Brit got a burger and a shake. We took our food to a comfy booth and, starving, I shoved fries into my mouth.

Brit, who'd taken a giant bite of her burger, saw the fries sticking out of my mouth and covered her mouth as she started to laugh.

"Stop!" I said, laughing too, but trying to swallow. "I'm so hungry!"

"Me too," Brit said, wiping her eyes. "I was just thinking how ridic we probably both looked right then."

"Point," I said. "I probably looked like Charm when he stuffs his face with hay."

We grinned at each other and went back to our lunches.

I looked up when I felt someone waiting at the counter staring at me.

Callie.

She took her bag and headed toward us.

"Good luck tomorrow," she said. Her comment seemed directed at both of us, not just Brit.

"Um, thanks," I said.

"You too," Brit said.

"I'm sure you'll do well for Canterwood's YENT team," Callie said.

And, with that, she walked out of The Sweet Shoppe. Brit and I looked at each other—neither of us having the right words.

20
KILLER DISTRACTION TECHNIQUE

"GOOD LUCK, EVEN THOUGH YOU SOOO DON'T need it," Paige said, hugging me. It was early Sunday morning, and I was dressed in my pre-show clothes: yoga pants and a hoodie. I wore my breeches and show shirt under my casual clothes in case Charm decided to sneeze on me, which he'd done before. Several times.

"Thanks, P," I said. "I keep telling myself that it's just a schooling show, but I'm so nervous because it's my first time as a YENT rider."

Paige let go of me and shook her head. "You should walk in there like you own the place because you *are* a YENT rider."

That made me smile. She was back to the old Paige this morning, and I felt comforted by that.

"Right," I said, taking a breath. I shouldered my bag with my show boots and pulled open our door. "Text you later!"

"Go, Team Sasha!" Paige cheered.

I made a "shhh!" motion with my finger. It was barely five in the morning, and everyone else on our floor was probably still asleep. But Paige had gotten up with me when my alarm had gone off, and she'd distracted me with entertainment gossip until I'd been ready to leave.

I tiptoed down the hallway and eased open the door. It was still black outside as I made my way across campus and walked to the stable. I looked up at the sky, focusing on a star.

This is superlame because it's not even a shooting star, but whatever, I told myself. *I wish I could do well at the show today. I don't even have to win—I just want to prove to Mr. Nicholson that he made the right choice in choosing me for the team.*

I stopped, closed my eyes for a second, then kept walking. The chilly air had made me alert and awake the second I stepped outside, and I shivered in my jacket. I couldn't wait for the sun to come up.

Lights blazed in the dark as I neared the stable. Mike, Doug, and Mr. Conner were all moving from rider to rider. I waved to a sleepy-looking Alison who was wrapping

Sunstruck's legs with blue wraps for the trailer ride over. She was keeping him in his stall instead of on crossties since the Arabian had a tendency to get nervous when he knew he was going to travel. But Alison's calm personality meshed with the Arabian's high-strung personality and the two were a perfect match.

"How's he doing?" I asked her. I reached over the stall door and rubbed Sunstruck's cheek. The Arabian's nostrils were flaring pink and the palomino was sweating even in the cool air.

"He's nervous, you can tell," Alison said. "But I know he'll be fine. After he's bandaged, I'm taking him away from the craziness of the stable. Mr. Conner told me to lead him up and down the lanes with Mike or Doug's help if I need it."

"That's a good plan," I said. "Let me know if you need help."

Alison smiled. "Thanks, Sash."

Julia had Trix on crossties and I ducked under them. The black mare was unfazed by the commotion of the stable, and she looked half-asleep as Julia groomed her. We traded quick smiles, and I headed for Charm's stall. I wanted to start waking him up before I got his tack.

"Hey, guy," I said, softly. "Time to wake up."

Charm's tail was to me and he had his head down in the corner. His hind leg was cocked and he was in a deep sleep.

"Charmy . . ." I called him a name I knew he hated.

He lifted his head and turned around to face me.

"Sorry," I said, trying not to laugh. "I know how much you hate that name. But I had to wake you up. I'll be right back with your tack and then we'll get you groomed and ready to go."

On my way down the aisle, I passed Callie. Like me, she was in sweats. She stared ahead, not saying a word or looking at me. In the tack room, I grabbed Charm's gear and put it on top of his trunk. Mike or Doug would load it in the storage bin in the trailer.

I reached Charm's stall and led him out. He'd stayed clean overnight, so it only took minutes for me to brush his body, pick his hooves, and run a comb through his mane and tail.

"Listen up, please," Mr. Conner called. "The trailers will be leaving in fifteen minutes. I suggest you start leading your horses out front so we can begin loading. It should take us about twenty minutes to get there, so no falling asleep on the ride over. " He smiled at us.

I tried to force my stomach to stop flip-flopping.

"Let's go, boy," I said to Charm. We walked outside, and I led him over to Brit who was waiting with Apollo.

"Is he a good traveler?" I asked Brit.

"The best," she said. "What about Charm?"

"Oh, he'll only sleep the entire twenty-minute ride."

We laughed and waited for our turn to have Mike or Doug load our horses.

Mike came and held out his hand for Charm's lead line. I kissed Charm's muzzle and handed the lead to Mike.

"See you there, boy."

Doug came and took Apollo from Brit, and we both climbed into the same truck, Brit sliding in next to Heather.

"Here we go," Heather said. "We've all got about twenty minutes to think about how we're going to win and not mess this up."

I shook my head at her. "Very inspiring pep talk, Heather. Thanks."

Heather flashed a cocky grin at me. "Oh, Silver. It wasn't a pep talk. It was a you-better-not-mess-up-on-my-team-or-I'll-have-to-hurt-you talk."

As much as I didn't want to, I laughed. Heather's attitude distracted me from being afraid.

21

FOUR, THREE,
TWO . . .

"HERE WE ARE," MIKE SAID, PULLING THE trailer onto the show grounds. There were hundreds of horses and riders everywhere—I'd never seen so many. Because it was a schooling show, riders of all age group and levels of riding had come to prep for show season. Mike pulled the trailer up to an empty parking spot and turned off the ignition. He got out of the truck, heading for the back to unload the horses.

"There are *so* many riders," I said, my voice squeaky.

Heather looked around Brit and glared at me. "Okay. Look. Half of them are, like, what? Under seven? The other half beginner and intermediate with *very* few YENT riders. You've probably seen *one* in this entire crowd. So shut up and get out of the truck."

"Okay, okay," I grumbled. But I was secretly glad for her not-so-scientific breakdown of the competition.

Brit, Heather, and I got our horses and headed to open stalls to groom and tack them up.

The three of us were ready in record time, and I pulled off my jacket and sweat pants. I looped Charm's reins around my arm and sat on an empty tack trunk, swapping my paddock boots for my show boots.

Mr. Conner met Heather, Brit, and me near the exit of the stable. "Take your time walking the course. Then, warm up your horses and then we'll head to the show jumping arena," he said. "The three of you have your jumping class first."

We all looked at each other. No one had known who was doing what. It hadn't exactly been a secret—but it had been unspoken.

"Let's go, competition," Heather said.

Making silly faces behind her back, Brit and I followed the signs to the show jumping arena. We were all riding for Canterwood, but in the arena, it was every girl for herself.

An hour and a half later it was show time. Mom and Dad had already called me twice, and I'd gotten good luck texts from Paige and Jacob. But now, my mind was all about the ride in front of me. Three other YENT riders, including Heather, had already gone. Heather and Aristocrat had pulled off a clear round and were holding the top spot. Everyone had knocked a rail except for her. Unless Brit or I went clear, she'd win.

"Up next, we have number three, Sasha Silver, on Charm," the announcer said. "Sasha is riding for Canterwood Crest Academy."

Charm shifted under me, ready to go.

I tried to stay loose in the saddle, waiting for the starting bell to go off.

Diiing! I didn't let Charm enter the ring the second he heard the bell. I waited a few more seconds, then let him into a canter. When I'd walked the course, I hadn't noticed anything too tricky about the seven jumps. It was a short course and, going with the theme of the show, it was all about easing the rider back into competition.

Charm's canter was even as he moved over the first vertical with black and white poles. He cleared it easily, and we cantered six strides toward an oxer. I gave Charm extra rein to clear the spread and he did without a problem. Wind whooshed in my ears as we cantered forward, Charm's ears pointing forward as he started to get excited.

Nope, keep him focused! I told myself. I did a half halt and got his attention back on me. We soared over another vertical with red poles and headed for a double combination. Charm leaped the first part of the jump, took a stride and then was airborne again over the second half. He cleared it with room to spare.

We made a sweeping turn around the giant arena, passing what felt like a thousand faces in the crowd. I gazed back between Charm's ears and watched as we approached the next jump—a faux stone wall. Charm rocked back on his haunches, then pushed up off the ground over the fake stone. I loved the feeling of being in the air, and I couldn't hold back my smile when we reached the ground.

Two left, I told myself. *Two! Left!*

The next two verticals were higher than any others on the course. I held my breath as I pointed Charm at the next-to-last vertical—a kind of scary-looking one with polka dots painted on it. But Charm didn't slow. He leaped high into the air and landed on the other side without coming close to touching it.

We were strides away from the final jump, and I started counting strides. *Five, four, three, two, one . . . no!*

Charm rushed forward and took off a second too early.

Caught off guard, I couldn't slow him. His front hooves clipped the top rail and it tumbled to the ground.

Disappointment surged through me, but I didn't let it show.

"Good job, boy," I said. And I meant it, even if I was upset at myself for not paying enough attention.

But I wasn't going to beat myself up about it. The show was over and I had plenty of time between now and the next show to practice.

"Good job, Silver," Heather said as I rode over by her.

"Thanks."

I dismounted and walked Charm in circles. Brit was next and I was excited to see her ride. As I walked Charm, the sadness I felt about knocking the rail disappeared. It was a schooling show, and we'd both learned from it.

I halted Charm as Brit approached the entrance. I crossed my fingers for her, wanting her to do well, but torn at the same time. If she had a clear round, she'd go to a jump-off with Heather and my current standing of third place would be knocked to fourth.

But we were all a team and I wanted her to do well.

"Our final rider for this class is Brit Chan on Apollo," the announcer said. "Brit is riding for Canterwood Crest Academy."

Brit sat still waiting for the bell. It dinged and she moved Apollo into a canter. The gelding moved toward the first jump, and I watched him carefully, just now seeing *something* was off.

"Is he—," I started to say.

"He's favoring his left foreleg," Heather said. "Oh, God."

Brit didn't feel it yet—she would have pulled him up if she did—but if she kept jumping him, Apollo could sustain a serious injury.

"Mr. Conner!" I called over to him. But he was already headed for the officials.

Brit and Apollo launched into the air, and I felt Heather grab my arm.

I could barely watch.

Apollo cleared the rail, looking gorgeous, with his mane and tail flowing as he flew over the jump. He hit the ground and looked as if he landed strong, then he wobbled, almost going down on his knees.

"Omigod," Heather and I said at the same time.

Brit tipped forward, losing a stirrup. But she managed to keep her seat. Apollo, loving Brit too much to quit, tried to keep cantering forward. He tossed his head, ignoring Brit's cue to stop and cantered three strides—hobbling on three legs.

Brit tugged on the reins and, finally, Apollo listened. He wasn't even at a complete stop when Brit flung herself out of the saddle and onto the ground to hold him still. Mr. Conner and an emergency veterinarian jogged toward them and a sobbing Brit buried her face in Apollo's mane.

I didn't hear the announcer or the crowd, I yanked my arm from Heather's grasp and ran toward Brit. Guilt almost knocked me over—if only I'd said something when I'd first noticed what I thought was lameness. None of this would be happening now.

"Brit," I said. "He's going to be fine."

Brit grabbed me and cried on my shoulder.

"He's going to be okay," Mr. Conner said. "Let's step back so the vet can examine him."

I held Brit's hand and Heather appeared beside her as we watched the vet test Apollo's hoof with tongs. The horse tried to move sideways when the vet pressed on a certain spot.

"What's wrong with him?" Brit asked. "Is he going to be okay? Please, please tell me he's okay."

The vet turned to us, while gently placing Apollo's hoof on the ground. "He's going to be absolutely fine. It's a bruised hoof, and with rest and icing, it will heal.

You did an excellent job in pulling him up before he could seriously injure himself."

Brit ran over and hugged Apollo's neck.

"Sasha, you and Heather take Brit back to school," Mr. Conner said. "Mike will drive you. We'll get Apollo bandaged for the ride home, and Doug will take care of Charm and Aristocrat."

"Okay," I said.

"No," Brit said. "I'm not leaving without him. I can't go."

"Brit," I said. "He'll be right behind us. Let's go back to school, get out of our show clothes, and then we'll be waiting for him when he gets home. Okay?"

"It's the best thing," Heather said. "The vet can work faster without the owner there—trust me. Apollo will be back in his stall within an hour and then you can stay there with him all day."

Brit wiped tears off her pale face. She stared at me, and when I nodded, finally said, "Okay."

With an arm around her shoulders, I led Brit back to the truck with Heather by my side.

22

AND ♦ ♦ SEND

WHEN MIKE DROPPED US OFF US, HEATHER and I walked Brit back to Orchard. We'd talked her down on the ride over and had done the best we could to convince her that she'd done nothing wrong. Heather didn't mention once that she'd won or that I'd come in third. It didn't matter. We were both doing everything we could to calm Brit.

Heather pulled open the door to Orchard and I followed Brit inside. She reached her room and unlocked the door. Brit sat on the edge of her chair, her head in her hands.

"I should have felt it in the warm-up," she said. "What kind of rider doesn't feel it when their horse is that lame?"

"Brit, don't," Heather said. "It's not your fault—don't

make me tell you that again. You pulled him up the *second* you felt something was off. If you would have had even the slightest feeling that something was wrong, you never would have shown him. Right?"

Brit nodded. "Right." She took a shaky breath. "And thankfully, it's a bruise. I know he's in pain and I *hate* that, but it could have been something serious."

"You're right," I said, sitting at the edge of her bed. "Callie's horse bruised his hoof last year and he made a full recovery. Apollo will too. Trust me. Mr. Conner will be right there supervising his recovery all the way."

That seemed to comfort Brit. She pulled off her show boots. "I can't thank you guys enough. I would have been a disaster if I'd had to ride back alone or with people I didn't know."

"Of course we want to help," I said. I got up and hugged her.

Heather nodded. "We'll do whatever we can to help Apollo get better."

Brit gave us a tiny smile. "Thanks, guys. I'm going to change and go put extra sawdust in his stall so it's extra padded when he gets here."

"I'm going to change and I'll be right down," I said.

"Me too," Heather added.

We left Brit's room and I headed to Winchester.

When I got to my own room, I opened the door and Paige was texting.

"You're back superearly," she said. "Is everything okay?"

"Brit's horse went lame on course," I said, tugging off my boots.

Paige covered her mouth. "Omigod. Is he okay?"

"It's a bruise, so it hurts, but he'll heal," I said. "I'm going to the stable to help Brit get him settled."

"That's really nice of you, Sash. I'm sure she appreciates it."

Paige's phone buzzed, and she read the text, then snapped it shut. Her fair cheeks turned pink.

"What's up?" I asked. "Is everything okay?"

Paige played with the ring around her index finger. "Yeah. Well. It was just Callie. We're going to the movies in a few."

I stopped pulling off my boot. "Oh. That's good. But."

"But what?"

I took a long breath. "You need to hear this from me. Callie's probably not going to have a great night tonight."

Paige looked at me, not saying anything. The way she was staring at me made me nervous. And words just started coming out.

"Paige, when I got back to school, I saw Jacob. And I didn't tell you. I saw him the first day I got back, and I was so afraid that you'd think I was losing focus again or jumping too fast from Eric to Jacob. I met him in the courtyard, and we decided to try getting back together."

I watched Paige's face, waiting for her to look shocked or angry or *something*. But her expression was blank just like Callie's had been whenever she'd talked to me this week.

"Jacob and I never got a chance to be together," I said. "Heather messed it up for us and then Callie happened, which wasn't her fault. And I did care about Eric—I still do—as a friend. But I have to try with Jacob, Paige. I have to."

I took another quick breath, wanting to say everything before Paige could get out a word.

"And that's why Callie's going to be upset tonight. She's going to need you as a friend because Jacob's going to tell her the truth about my birthday party. He's going to tell her that he tried to kiss me and I made him lie to protect her from being hurt. I can't even imagine what Callie's going to feel."

I stopped, unable to take another breath or say another word. I just couldn't.

Paige stared at me for what felt like hours. "Sasha," she

said. I braced myself. Waiting for her to tell me it was a bad idea. Waiting for her to say I had to stop Jacob from telling Callie.

"What?" I managed to get out.

"Callie already knows."

Paige said the sentence without any emotion. Just . . . calm.

No. No-no-no. I said to myself. I had to have heard Paige wrong.

"You didn't—you said—no. Callie doesn't—no."

"She knows," Paige said. "Because I told her."

I looked at my best friend as if I'd never seen her before.

"What?" I almost screamed. "How could you do this to me?"

"I'm her friend too," Paige said. "She needed someone."

"But you kept this from *me*. I'm your best friend. I-I don't even know how you could do something like this and just not tell me!"

Paige half smiled. "Kind of like how you kept your meeting with Jacob from me."

I almost fell off my bed. This couldn't be happening. I couldn't be losing another best friend. It was too much.

Without looking at Paige, I dug through my purse and grabbed my phone. My fingers shook as I typed a text.

Still need a roommate?

And then I pressed send.

FIVE GIRLS. ONE ACADEMY. AND SOME SERIOUS ATTITUDE.

CANTERWOOD CREST

by Jessica Burkhart

TAKE THE REINS

CHASING BLUE

BEHIND THE BIT

TRIPLE FAULT

BEST ENEMIES

LITTLE WHITE LIES

RIVAL REVENGE

HOME SWEET DRAMA

Don't forget to check out the website for downloadables, quizzes, author vlogs, and more!
www.canterwoodcrest.com